DREAM
BOOK
Unikirja

DREAM
BOOK
Unikirja

K. A. Laity

www.foxspirit.co.uk

Dreambook: Unikirja © 2015 K.A. Laity
p213 contains additional copyright acknowledgments

Cover Art © 2015 S.L. Johnson
http://sljohnsonimages.com/

Second Edition (previously published by Aino Press)

conversion by handebooks.co.uk

ISBN: 978-1-909348-75-2

Published by:
Fox Spirit Books
www.foxspirit.co.uk
adele@foxspirit.co.uk

CONTENTS

To my ancestors

KIITOS (*THANKS*)

Kiitos paljon to Gerry Henkel, kantele-maker extraordinaire, who crafted my very first kantele, Louhi. As editor of *New World Finn*, Gerry was a constant supporter for this project including publishing several of the stories in *New World Finn*'s pages.

Kiitos and warm hugs to Minna Popkin and Kasha Breau, my fellow members of Louhi's Daughters. Not only is it a lot of fun singing, storytelling, and playing the kantele together, but our initial performance of the Aino story helped give birth to this project. Kasha proved to be a wonderful kantele teacher, and my playing advanced so much with her help. Let's have another reunion soon!

Kiitos to all the fine folks at the Finnish American Heritage Society in Canterbury, Connecticut for hosting Louhi's Daughters in our various incarnations and for connecting me with friends who share the interest in keeping Finnish heritage a living link between us all.

Kiitos to the lovely ladies at Still Point Interfaith Retreat, where I spent a blissfully silent week working on the play, 'Lumottu,' in January 2008.

Kiitos to the folks who comprised the first Mythic Journeys conference, an inestimable well of inspiration still echoing in my mind, especially Ulla Suokko, Anya Martin and Phil Nutman.

Kiitos to Sarah Cummings-Ridge and everyone at the Maine Kantele Institute. You helped my playing improve so much, so quickly. The kantele building workshop unlocked the mysteries of the instrument in my hands, while the nightly jam sessions and sing-a-longs gave us all a lot of laughs.

Kiitos paljon to the Writers' Colony at Dairy Hollow, my warm home for a month when I won the 2005 Eureka! Short Story Fellowship. You offered me a beautiful sanctuary where I wrote so much, saw turtles everywhere, and shared the fellowship of other writers over delicious meals.

Kiitos paljon to the Finlandia Foundation for the 2006 grant which gave me the priceless opportunity to visit the rock paintings around Finland's Saimaa Lake. Thanks to Anya Martin for arranging for me to meet her cousin Laura Jalkanen-Lehtinen and her lovely family, who all welcomed me like a long-lost relative and showed me the beauties of fabulous Helsinki.

Kiitos to all the friends who have listened to me read and perform these stories over the long years of composition and offered encouragement and thoughtful criticism, particularly Mildred L. Perkins and Susan Simko, Pat Golemon, all the Connecticut crew and my cousins in Finland.

Paljon kiitoksia to Gene Kannenberg, Jr., who prepared the first Aino Press edition in 2009.

Paljon kiitoksia to Adele Wearing and Fox Spirit Books for breathing new life into this project!

K. A. Laity

Hudson, New York

October 2014

Mythic
Visions

This little tale is based on an ancient story retold the world over. I gave it a particularly Finnish cast by featuring folkloric favorites, the beloved cuckoo and the clever raven.

Raven Sister, Cuckoo Sister

Raven sister sits on the branch of the long-needled pine. Cuckoo sister sits below at her loom, weaving the world into being, hands in motion, always in motion.

Raven sister says, come away with me, we will fly across the forests, skim through the trees, reach the high mountain peaks. Cuckoo sister says, you know I cannot, I am weaving the world into being.

Raven sister sighs and says, come away with me, we will soar over the lakes, cross the salty oceans, and see the giant pike in the depths of the sea. Cuckoo sister says, you know I cannot, I am weaving the world into being.

The golden marten comes by with tears on her whiskers. Help me find my kits, she says, they have strayed from our burrow and are lost.

Raven sister laughs and says, they will come home when they are hungry and tired. She pays no more attention, but preens her pretty wings. Cuckoo sister says, I will help, and takes her bird form to fly over the treetops.

Raven sister flies down from the branches and takes the shuttle in her snapping beak. She pulls and pulls until the weaving comes undone. Just before the world is undone, cuckoo sister returns.

Who has pulled the shuttle out, she asks her raven sister. I don't know, the other answers, it must have been the fox. Cuckoo sister takes up the shuttle and begins again to weave the world into being.

Just then the hare arrives, rubbing her paws nervously. There are hunters in the woods, she says, will you help me find their snares.

Raven sister chuckles and says, run through the bushes and you will find them soon enough. She pays no more attention, but only preens her gleaming chest. Cuckoo sister says, I will help, and once more takes her bird shape and flies away through the woods.

Raven sister goes to the loom and catches a weight on her beak. She tosses it away and the weave begins to curl. She takes another and another, but just before the world becomes undone, cuckoo sister returns.

Who has taken all my loom weights, she asks her raven sister. I don't know, the other answers, it must have been the squirrel. Cuckoo sister finds the weights and begins once more to weave the world.

Next the bear turns up, a frown across her brow. I cannot find a hive of bees anywhere, she says, will you help me find some honey.

Raven sister cackles and says, why then you'll have to go without. She pays no more attention, but only preens her shimmering tail. Cuckoo sister says, I will help, and takes her bird form to fly across the meadows.

Raven sister pulls the heddle out from the loom and the weft begins to loosen. She pulls and pulls, and the fabric starts to unravel. Just before the world becomes undone, cuckoo sister returns.

Who has taken my heddle, she asks her raven sister. I don't know, the other answers, it must have been the troll. Cuckoo sister finds the heddle and begins again to weave the world.

And so it goes, every day somewhere in the Finnish woods. Cuckoo sister weaves the world, while raven sister tries to pull it apart. When cuckoo weaves the world, all is well and happy. When raven pulls at the warp and weft, everything falls apart. One day good, the next bad, always back and forth. If ever either one completes her task, the world will be no more.

This poem came from a dream—and perhaps a lingering memory of Angela Carter's The Bloody Chamber. *I always saw it as being a late-night performance accompanied by traditional Finnish shamanic drumming and nature's soft voices.*

WOLF SISTER

(WITH DRUM AND NIGHT SOUNDS)

I AM THE WOLF SISTER
     running at your side.
Each of us knows
     our roles in the hunt.
Pack politics are plain
     and often bloody.
Scarred pads whisper
     across the moonlit plains
As the caribou lows
     uncontrolled panic.
Stars blink, mute witnesses
     to the pursuit.

I am the wolf sister
     springing for the throat,
As your jaws close
     on the trembling haunch.
Elder sister settles for
     a tenuous grip on tendons.
Little brother growls
     and seeks a tender target,
But mother ducks in low,
     cracking the fragile knee
And the horned one arcs
     down in a spray of white.

I am the wolf sister

    painting my mouth red,

Ripping the soft windpipe

    from the wet vermillion silence.

My belly rounds quickly,

    stuffed with stolen warmth.

My satisfaction swells

    with our splattered tableau;

I raise my muzzle high

    and sing to distant lupine gods.

My pack's voice joins in

    the canticle of sanguine delight.

This is the first of the stories I wrote, inspired by the 'Aino' story from runos 3-5 of the Kalevala. *It has become a kind of touchstone for the collection, for the story of Aino's watery suicide runs like a recurring tune through these tales. Aino avoids marriage to the ancient sage Väinämöinen by throwing herself into a watery grave, but she returns as a salmon to shame him for trying to force a young beauty into wedlock. This tale set the tone for this collection which focuses on women's experience of the world—an aspect so often missing from the original* Kalevala *stories.*

DARKEST DAY

SHE WAS A SACRIFICE. NOT BECAUSE SHE WAS PURE—THOUGH THAT SHE WAS—but because she was their best. She would bring much fame to her family, for she would be their second offering. Many long winters before, her sister Sari had gone. 'Sari is with the Winter Giant,' Mama had often said to the little ones, smiling while her eyes sorrowed. And now Arja must go too, and add to the sadness in her mother's heart.

The village had honored them all. The hunters had insisted that Arja choose from the best of each kill. Old Pekka had grumbled by with a skin of his berry liqueur, mumbling a grudging word of thanks to Papa before stomping off into the snow. Linne had crafted a fine necklace of jangling bones and reindeer horn and shiny bright blue stones that lit up the twin gems of Arja's eyes. The elders had walked all together one night to present her with a fine bearskin cloak. Her papa had crowed over its thick pelt, holding it aloft so Arja and her mama could trace the fine stitches embroidered on the inside. Three scenes told the story of Aino, the salmon maiden—her spurning of old Väinämöinen, and her watery death, and her final transformation into the fish. This cloak was her people's treasure. Arja had thanked them humbly, blushing with terror and enjoyment, even as she wondered to herself how much good it would do her in the Winter Giant's realm. But she took it gratefully—such a prize! Papa had swelled with pride. 'Even Sari did not receive such a magnificent gift,' he had said, pulling playfully at her long braids. Arja had glowed as if the fire reflected in her cheeks had caught and burned. She had loved to clap the bear paws together under her chin and hear the claws clack.

That sound was less enjoyable as she waited alone on the frozen tundra, the many gifts surrounding her under the three-sided tent they had left her within. The open side faced north. He would come from there, Arja knew. The preparations had been careful. After rising long before their men would stir, her mother and the other women had led Arja to the sauna for a careful cleansing. They had beat her skin with the birch twigs until she felt the pleasant glow of well-being, as the steam belched up with each ladle of cold water poured upon the hot rocks. Arja could almost forget why she was being so pampered. Mamma had weaved red and white ribbons in her hair, braiding the colors into her waist-length plaits. The women had helped her slip into the beautiful red dress they had all had a hand in making—Mari's fine stitching, Linne's beads, Hanni's weaving—and pulled on the warm fur boots that had belonged to the eldest of the elders. Fine silver bells ringed the ermine tops and jangled when she walked.

These bells rang out across the plains as Arja stamped her feet to keep warm; soon her little chimes were answered with further ringing from the north. She squinted into the darkness, trying to find movement within the white. If the sun were rising, Arja thought, I would be able to see him. But on this day the sun did not rise. Hiisi had taken it away, further and further, until darkness fell upon their land without respite—as he did every winter. And I have been chosen to appease him. Arja clacked the bear claws together under her chin and felt her heart beat faster.

Now she could see a shape against the drifts. The steady chime of the approaching bells melted into Arja's thoughts until she could no longer hear it. The occasional crack of a whip, urging some beast on, ran through her head and snapped through her body. Closer now. The animal drawing the sled seemed to be an elk of immense proportions, but there was something odd to it. As it plunged through the wind-sculpted banks layering the plain and covered the distance with surprising speed, Arja puzzled at the beast's strange silhouette. When it was yards away, she could make out the yellow eyes that twinkled like lilies on the pond's surface, the head like a stump rotted by winter's cruelty and crowned with a broken branch, the legs that ran so fast, leaping through the snow, and looked like saplings or maybe fence posts. The pelt of this creature now pulling up before her appeared to be as rough as the bark of a fir, winter-hardened and wind-teased. Could such a thing truly be alive? This sorcery made her shudder.

But Arja's wide eyes had not yet even taken in the one who had conjured such an alarming creature into being. He was taking her in, though. As he threw down his whip and shook off several layers of white bear skins, his eyes—dark as a night-flying raven—hungrily swallowed her body. Arja felt faint. He was so tall! And his shoulders hunched with power, like twin eels ready to spring. White hair rippled out the sides of his cap, but it brought her no comfort—this was no grandfather. The Winter Giant stepped down from his sleigh, accompanied by a ringing as the massive elk shook his traces, pawing at the snow. Arja's body was a river of trembles that shook music from her boots and tears from her eyes.

A foot away now, he looked down upon Arja, then shifted his gaze to the goods behind her. At last, a smile. The Giant moved with surprising speed—and grace. He crowed like a small boy, delighted with the fresh-baked breads, the exquisitely smoked meat—Matti used special herbs along with the birch twigs to flavor the reindeer flesh—and of course, Pekka's berry drink. He lifted the skin above his head and squeezed the fermented juice into his gaping jaws. Such sharp teeth! And so many! Arja gulped, but her mouth remained dry.

It took him scant minutes to load the sleigh. It had taken half the village to bring all the gifts out here in the darkness, then leave one by one—Mamma holding on as if she might not leave, until she too had turned away and walked off into the night. The Winter Giant carried armfuls to the sleigh, piling them quickly, but with care, so nothing would be damaged in the ride back. He did not ask her help, so Arja stood silently by. The loading done, he rubbed his hands—paws? They were so rough, the nails so long and sharp—together with satisfaction and turned to Arja.

'Well, my bride, it is time we go.'

Arja took his offered hand, her toes curling under as her small fingers were grasped by his frigid ones. Their cold was a new shock, even after the hours alone in the tent on the plains. A cold that came from within, from his cold heart, no doubt, Arja thought. How can I bear this? But she was already seated beside him and he was drawing the white bear skins over their laps. He paused to run his fingers over her own bear skin cloak. 'Not bad for such a little creature.' Again he laughed, smiling down at Arja. The smile was terribly frightening. Arja could only think of how those teeth would feel in the morning.

'What are you thinking, my bride?'

Arja opened her mouth, but no sound came out at first. She swallowed. 'I was wondering what it will feel like to be in Tuonela.'

Again the Giant roared with laughter. 'You will not go to the Land of the Dead, child. When I eat you, I eat your spirit. Why do you think I am so strong? How can I pull the sun so far from your land? I eat spirits of human folk! Tasty they are!' His teeth scraped together as he spoke, like knives on bone.

Though warm under all the bear skins, Arja felt chilled to her heart. She had resigned herself to death. Someone had to die after all, for the good of the tribe—and there was honor in it. But to be consigned to oblivion! Trapped forever in the brutish hulk of this ogre—no, no, that she had not prepared for. Sitting next to the great giant as he urged on the huge elk with growls and whipcracks, Arja strained to hear the lost souls trapped within him. To be so cut off from the world of the living—she could not fathom it. There had been some comfort in the thought that Mamma would be able to call forth Arja's spirit from the grave already laid for her, the grave without a body. Only a lock of her hair, braided then cut off—only that was buried in the hollow with the other folk of their tribe. A scree of carefully chosen stones marked the place where her body would not lie. A shiver had run through her then, too, but it was balanced with the thought that her spirit might commune with family again at that spot. We go on, Papa always said. But Sari was always 'with the Winter Giant.' Had they known? Then why make her a grave?

'You are silent,' the giant said gruffly, pausing to wipe his streaming nose.

'I am unhappy,' Arja said.

The big teeth gaped wide once more as he threw his head back laughing. When he stopped, the big grey eyes regarded

Arja perplexedly. 'Well, at least you are quiet. Usually they cry and scream. Quiet is good.' And without another word they rode for hours, with only the elk's jingling traces to break the silence of the windswept plains.

The Winter Giant's home was a cleft in a cliff that opened into an immense cavern. One would never find it in the landscape's vast blankness without knowing just where to look. Arja watched as the giant released the elk, who shook his head and ran for the edge of the forest to make his dinner of what he could paw from the drifts. Just as easily as before, the great ogre carried all the precious gifts deep into the cave, motioning with a jerk of his head that Arja should follow within. A merry fire burned there, as if determined to cheer the poor girl, but still she shivered.

Here I will die, Arja thought glumly. She was too tired even to work up any anger or to fight. What could she possibly do against such a foe? Her eyes followed him. He was pawing through all the gifts with a child-like eagerness that somehow made his powerful frame that much more menacing. He could hurl her against the wall as easily as a boy might throw a snowball. And then eat her. It was too much.

'Here.' The Winter Giant had opened all the packages and finally settled on the liqueur, some of the braided breads, as well as the pickled herring in the earthenware jar. He held out a piece of bread to her, ripped from a loaf. His claws held it fast. She hesitated. He laughed. 'Yes, have some!' Gingerly, Arja reached for the bread, sure that the claws would dart out and stab her hand, but he released the piece of bread and it dropped into her tiny palm. 'Well, how do you like your wedding night.'

'Will there be no ceremony even?'

'What does it matter? You are only food, in the end.'

'It matters to me. I am offered by my people as your bride—that I must perish after is not my concern. But the ritual is very important to me.'

'Well, you may leap over the fire if you wish. I believe your people do such a thing.' The giant chuckled as if this were very funny. 'Then are we married?'

Arja stood up and felt the prickly skin of her legs as the blood began to flow sluggishly. 'It will do.'

It should have been such a joyful moment. Her family

should have been around her, her village. Some young man should have been standing on the other side of the fire—not this great hairy beast of a creature, gnawing his way through her people's precious goods as the water sweated down the ice of the cavern. The fire should have been a symbol of blessing and fertility, filling her with the potential fruitfulness that their harsh life demanded. But here she was in the cave of the Winter Giant, his wife, his food. Let there be some blessing in this, Arja thought, eyes closed. Mother Sun, may your presence return to my people and this fire warm my heart and spirit. After a moment's reflection, she gathered her skirts and leapt over the crackling flames. The orange and yellow fingers reached up as if to caress her sturdy legs, and buoyed Arja with a warm pillow of heat. She landed on the other side, her mind buzzing with half-formed thoughts. So I am married, so our souls entwine, until death claims one. Must it be me? Arja regarded her husband without emotion. 'It is done. Now you will return the sun to my people?'

'It is already done,' the giant mumbled with a mouth full of herring. 'The sun is returning, a little more each day.' Again his raucous laughter echoed through the cave. 'You can know my secret now. I do not control the sun. She moves on her own. Her yearly path takes her far from this land, but she always returns. Your foolish people! One very very bad, harsh winter, they believed the bragging words of this one,' he thumped his chest proudly. 'So now they pay me, and I eat when the sun is farthest and the nights are coldest and game scarce. I eat well—tender young flesh.'

Arja burned, her eyes grew flames and her heart sizzled.

'None of the others asked, you know. Terrified they were. No wedding, no fire jumping. Just tears. Is it better knowing? No,' he cackled, 'I can see it is not.'

Arja's blood raged through her flesh, her anger gathering momentum. But she could not strike out—what good would it do? Make him roar with laughter all the more? No, she could not attack him. In Arja's heart, the hot rage turned to cold tin. The questions inspired by her leap over the fire continued to whip through her thoughts. She did not even realize there was a smile on her face—grim as it was—as she turned to the giant once more. 'Husband, may I ask a boon of you?'

'You know, you may call me 'Hiisi,' as you are my wife— for now.' He smiled over the skin of berry liqueur, his lips stained red. Arja felt a deeper chill, realizing how he would look with her blood splashed across his greedy mouth. 'You may ask a boon of me—provided you do not ask to be spared death.'

'I shall not ask that. But as I am never to rest in the land of the dead, may I at least be allowed to see Tuonela once before I die? Surely that is not so much to ask.'

'Hmmph,' Hiisi grunted. He was quite comfortable sitting cross-legged upon his bear skins, the many gifts gathered around him. Clearly he had no desire to make such a journey. 'There is little to interest anyone there. And you could only stand on the shore. I could not take you into the land itself. My power is not such.'

Arja controlled her smile. It must not look happy, only ingratiating. 'This is all I ask. It is not so much. After tonight I shall see nothing. Let me have one glimpse of the land from which my ancestors speak to us.'

Hiisi considered her request as he chomped on the salty fish, stopping occasionally to slurp at his claws. 'I suppose there is no harm in it. But there is little of interest in it either. You will be disappointed.' He looked at Arja, her chin jutted out implacably, and sighed. 'But I cannot refuse a final request from my delicious wife.'

He sighed and put down his treats, with a careful pat, as if to bid them wait his return. Arja bundled her cloak around her shoulders once more, her eyes brightly eager. Hiisi stretched, wiped his jaws with a huge paw, and belched noisily. This made him laugh even more loudly. His young wife smiled agreeably, but her thoughts already ranged ahead: Tuonela! Never would she have thought that so much hope could dwell in the Land of the Dead.

If her journey to the ice cliffs had been swift, then she had no suitable word for the speed of her second ride. Arja struggled to stay upright as the sled whistled over the icy banks. The white skins shifted with every bounce, and her teeth chattered with the cold and terror. But she must be

brave. It had been her choice to come, to face once more
the pallid expanses and the rattling winds, to risk what little
life she had left. Tears flowed freely down Arja's cheeks. Even
she could not tell whether they sprang from the whips of
frigid air or from her fears. She was going to die, Arja knew
it truly now. But the question still hung before her: How?

Just at the horizon, white turned to black, a darkness that
was yet not so dark as that overhead. With alarm Arja saw
that the first presages of dawn—not that they would actually see the sun that day—had whispered across the sky. The
heavens were still black, but no longer the dark of a raven's
wing. Hurry, hurry, she silently urged the bark elk, who—
as if he had heard her plea—seemed to have saved a final
burst of energy to reach this far-off goal. Through her tears
Arja could see the dark lake, its sooty surface broken only by
the wake of a gliding swan, and in its center, a whirlpool's
hungry swirl. Tuonela, the land of the dead: beyond the
mist she could not see, but she knew in the center an island
lay. No one knew how big or small, even those who dwelled
there. Some things could not be known.

'Well, my wife,' Hiisi roared too loud for the silent
shores, as he pulled hard at the elk's reins. 'Here is your land
of dead. We must hurry back now, it is time to eat!' But Arja
was already clambering down from her seat, squirming out
from under the bear skins. Hiisi stared, his mouth hanging
open. Arja looked into his eyes. For the first time all fear
fled from her heart, and she saw her own truth. He cannot
guess. 'Aino, salmon maiden, share your gift,' she muttered. 'Help me escape Hiisi as you escaped your would-be
husband.' Then she turned and ran toward the clouded
banks. Hiisi gave a yelp of surprise, threw aside his whip,
and hopped down from the sled. But he was not so fast
this time. He would not catch her. She did not even try to
shake off her heavy clothes, her beautiful boots, the clanking necklace that chivvied her throat. She only ran. Her feet
felt light and swift. Arja spread her arms as she approached
the water's edge, and the swan—as if in sympathy with her
flight—spread its wings too, and hissed a threat to any who
might stop her, raising up from the water and arching its
neck.

From the bank, Arja jumped. Her body arced, palms

together now; she hit the water like a leaping pike and plunged into the black spiral whirling down from the surface. Cold, so cold—and she had thought the midwinter air frozen! It was nothing to the glacial grasp of the midnight waters, fingers of ice that wormed through her garments and probed into her soul. I am dying, Arja realized. Her dive seemed to gain momentum, as if the whirlpool were greedily drawing her to its heart. Down and down she spun, losing all sense of direction, feeling her life slip away with her discarded clothes. Arja's eyes remained open, but she saw only her memories against the inky depths. Her life was all disappearing, washing away, trailing behind her, perhaps bursting at the surface. She did not even notice when the last bubbles of air left her nostrils, for the force of the water drew her on imperiously, until she saw nothing but blackness and felt no cold on her skin. Like a stone, Arja hit the bottom with a soft thump. Unlike a stone, though she flipped and nosed her way toward the surface, a strong tail propelling her up once more. Long before she breached the water's skin, Arja could see vague clouds stretching across the sky. It was the first midwinter dawn.

Arja leapt from the water, droplets dappling her new scales. It was a shock to slam down on the surface, gasping for air, then remembering, diving once more to pull the rich liquid through her gills. It was cold and pure and invigorating. But she had to go up one final time. She twisted around, trying to get her bearings. There, over there! Arja paddled her fins vigorously to keep her head above the waves, and looked back at her husband. Hiisi had fallen to his knees at the very place where she had leaped. It was not anger she heard in his voice now, only a terrible sadness. He would have eaten me, Arja reminded herself as she plunged back into her new watery world. Yet his aching cry followed her down. 'But you will tell them!'

Yes, her eyes told him. The dead can speak, while those consumed are wordless. I will appear in dreams, I will tell them.

'And then I will be alone!' Hiisi wailed. 'Alone!'

Yes, the salmon thought, as she flipped herself around, ready to journey. All alone.

When I first learned the story of the peasant Lalli who killed Bishop Henri (the cleric who brought Christianity to Finland), I was struck first by the misogyny of the original Kanteletar *ballad. Blaming Lalli's wife for his actions always felt suspiciously one-sided to me. So here I imagine another version of the story seen from the perspective of Lalli's wife, Kerttu, who has to live with her husband's crime and her own silence about the truth.*

Kerttu

The mice have not gone. It had not been our winter stores that drew them in, as we first thought. They do not even seem interested in food. I put bread outside the door. I thought it would draw them away, outside, but they do not leave. 'The mice have not gone,' I tell Lalli, but he ignores me and hunches lower over his gruel. He knows. It is he they are after.

At first we did not notice how many there were. There are always some. No matter how good a housekeeper you are (and I am very good, Mama saw to that), the mice will come. One day you pick up your bag of flour and out pours the milky stream from the hole they have chewed. Sometimes there's a tail, glimpsed quickly—so quickly you are not even sure you saw it—disappearing behind the stove. Mostly there are the droppings, little black pellets to be swept into the bucket and tossed out the window into the flower bed. But never so many as now.

The first time, I had just come back in from getting a bucket of water for the morning meal. The rain barrel had frozen over, so I trudged down to the lake's edge where the spring flows. The cold handle had clung to my fingers as if trying to share its misery as I heaved it down into the icy crust. The cold water had splashed up from the bucket, the drops also objecting to the frigid air. My lips and fingertips had become numb as my arm stretched down, while the wind fondled my cheek with unpleasant familiarity. The bitter cold off the lake's frozen surface was always cutting, always fierce—you could not get used to it. You merely withstood it for as long as the chores held you there.

My body had curled into a fist-like retreat by the time I returned to the door. The wind fought me for the latch-knob, roaring with laughter. His wind, no doubt. I jerked the door open at last and, with some considerable trouble, slammed it behind me, sloshing cupfuls of water to floor. Then I gasped. A hundred little mice, maybe more, maybe two hundred—they covered the table, a seething sea of tiny rodents, all rushing over one another in their excitement at having been discovered, trying to escape the blows they knew would come. Yet I was so astonished I could do nothing but stare slack-jawed while the bucket swung in my hands, its own tide running up the wooden sides, as if the lake too would take over our house. Mice are no strangers to me, to any of us, but so many—! Fear clamped onto my guts like the jaws of a wolf. It was wrong. It was magic: his magic.

But that wasn't the worst of it. That was just the first time. The worst was in bed. Maybe two nights later, the last full moon—it's waning tonight, almost to nothing, to darkness—when it was at its highest and I had already been asleep for some time, I awoke to the sound... What sound? Rustling? Crawling? Mice make no real noise. I guessed it was Lalli's groans.

At first even he did not wake. Their teeth, so tiny, so sharp, and yet—he must have thought he was dreaming. Horrid, horrid dreams of the pricks of their mouths on his flesh as he lay there, thrashing and moaning. Then he was waking and screaming and we beat them away, shaking the feather bed, throwing the pillows on the floor, across the room, the mice's small bodies tumbling. Those who survived skittered across the planks, dashing under the door and into the corners. Lalli shrieked, and that frightened me more than the mice. I finally calmed him with vinegar and water, a handful of dried herbs. I washed his wounds and the mixture stung, but that pain was familiar, expected. Lalli grew quiet, muttering angrily, but no longer shrieking.

The bites covered his right shoulder and back. How long had they been gnawing? How long were they in our bed? And why did they not bite me? I should have been grateful, but instead I was horror-struck. Did that one who caused all this still intend to get his boon? It sickened me.

Today, in the bluish light of the almost-dawn, I rose, determined to keep this enemy at bay. While the porridge bubbles over the fire and Lalli cares for horses and the cows, I turn my thoughts over Mama's recipes, counting them one by one on the threads of my belt, as if the real secrets might be buried within the knots. The magic of the old ways: When I was a child, Mama would visit the other women when she had no recipe or chant or song for a situation. Sooner or later we found someone who knew the right incantation, or the right mixture of herbs, though occasionally we had to walk many miles and stay in strange beds, or even just sleep in the hay. She usually dragged me behind her, pushing me into a corner to shuck peas or grind grain or peel potatoes while she memorized the song or the list of ingredients, only then trusting it to a new knot on her belt.

When I began to bleed she at last allowed me to learn the charms and the potions. By then I stood at her shoulder and repeated time and again the patient words, the careful concoctions. Long lists of herb, complicated procedures—tinctures, salves, and poultices—I had to learn them all. I had to repeat each one three times perfectly for Mama before she would let me add a new knot to my own red belt. When we gathered in the kitchens with the others, the crones would cackle with delight as my Mama had me rehearse the recipes, proud she could pick at knot at random and I would launch into my recital without the least hesitation. All those old women, sun-wrinkled, wind-kissed, now gone. The few women left in this blasted landscape, those not driven away by the screeching winds or the endless snow—sometimes still evident even in the brightness of Midsommar—too many follow the new ways, *his* magic.

I spit into the fire. I cannot comprehend it even now. His magic of pain and suffering—where was the appeal? An invisible world in the sky full of gold and bright music, he promised them, but only once you die. 'And now,' I asked my brother Hannu once, 'and now what? To make a virtue of our suffering, obtaining credits in the world in his world of clouds? What about now—as we suffer and struggle? Can his gods—no, god—not help us now?' Hannu had shrugged, as much convinced by the man's gold as by his stories. New stories, that was the thing; how long since we have had new stories around here? So they would invite him to supper, they would give him their pledges and they would be rewarded with gold and the little crossed sticks, reminders of a god who suffered—who makes his people repeat his agony.

Not for me; better to turn to Ahti and Vellamo, even if

they seem a bit morose at times. Their watery realm provides us with food all year, and they do not ask us to suffer each day, only to do our part. The fish do not leap into our cooking pot after all. But to say toil is the nature of the world is not to say we make a virtue of our pain. Pain is pain—it is not to be delighted in. Lessened, yes, avoided whenever possible, and healed when it must be endured—which brings me back once more to considering Lalli's condition.

It was no trouble finding a good poultice for his scalp. It soothed the pain and stanched the flow of blood quickly. But the hair will not grow. His pink flesh still looks raw and remains sensitive to touch. I try to keep him from picking at the livid scars, but he scowls when I slap his hand, for he does not even notice that he worries the flesh. If only he had not put the hat upon his head, that hat so full of that one's magic. But, no, Lalli had to crow, he had to boast—because of course he was so frightened by what he had done. My Lalli is not a violent man. As husbands go, he has been very tolerant. He rarely hits me and only when I have really tried his patience or been especially stubborn. I am stubborn. I know what is the wise thing to do, usually. But Mama told me years ago, wisdom goes out the window when a man has made up his mind about something. Better not to fight. Just clean up the mess when he's done. So I cleaned the mess when Lalli finally got tired of boasting, pulling the red cap off along with a generous stripe of hair and skin. He roared with pain and surprise and I rushed to get a cloth to stop the blood, a measure of ale to dull the throbbing hurt, and a jar of soothing cream to help the scalp heal. But my magics were not strong enough.

So he sits at night by the table, the flickering fire dancing before him, bathing his form in fingers of light and dark while he touches his head gingerly or contemplates his missing finger. The ring, too; that was a bad idea. He should have known. More magic. But gold, we all know the worth of it. And this ring was heavy with potential wealth. How many cows, how many horses—it was hard to calculate. I understood his desire to own it, even as I knew that I would do nothing with that man's magic except bury it deep in the earth or toss it to the bottom of Ahti's lake. Lalli agreed afterward, chopping through the ice with his axe, but even then it was too late. And then the mice came.

I stir the porridge and contemplate the possible removers I can concoct. Salt perhaps, the most efficient; but these are no ordinary mice. Regular mice would have taken the first few hints and moved on, never mind that this is the middle of winter. Normal mice never would have come nosing around all together like that, with so few pickings in midwinter. Burrowed in their little dens, they would be safe and warm. These have gathered from who knows where, trekked across ice and snow to gather here, to plague my Lalli. Unnatural. They have been charmed. That one's ghost must still be here, and I shiver now too. The tendrils of chill air that wrap around me: Drafts? Or his frosty touch? If I drive him out, will they go too? But what if his hat and his ring call him? They are on the bottom of the lake. I cannot destroy the physical remnants. Perhaps Ahti and Vellamo can be persuaded to help, to drive this spirit from their realm.

I still can see that day yet in my mind, pictures that run in a constant stream like a dream. His cheerful good humor and brash carelessness. Here was a man unaccustomed to having the least concern what anyone else thought. He had all the right answers. Lalli had gone that day to help Hannu break up some fallen trees. The winds had been fierce all night, whistling wild tunes for our sleep, prying their fingers through the planks and the mud. Hannu came early, wrapped in his bearskin, stomping loudly to let us know he had arrived. I sent the men on their way after steaming bowls of hot bread soup, Hannu especially pleased. As he has no wife, his meals are poor and tasteless, yet he refuses to live here and eat my meals more than once in a while. He lives like a bear himself, snuffling through the woods, seeking game and digging roots. Stubborn, my family, like we ought not be.

Barely had their steps filled with snow when I heard a sledge approaching. I did not know the commanding man in the sledge, but I knew what the big gold cross on his chest meant. The words had come through other means, whispered in corners or shouted across tables depending on one's confidence in the new ways. Gold paved the way as he made

the rounds of our region. Even Hannu had succumbed to
his words. No one really knew what it was, but I recognized
it for magic, a new kind of magic, so I was curious. And
now here was the man himself at my doorstep. He rapped
on the door with his walking stick, shouting out a halloo. I
greeted him and asked his name and his people. He cheer-
fully told me his name was Henrik, but he said I should call
him by his title, *Biskup*. His people lived far to the west and
spoke a different tongue. He removed his red hat and suggested I should kiss his ring because he came from the king
of Sweden who sent his greetings. I said I would kiss his
ring if he would kiss mine, but he does not seem to know
that saying, and I let it pass. He asked for some hay for his
horse as I put a bowl of soup before him, and I was happy to
oblige. Company this time of year is such a rare thing, what
is a little hay to share? I was sure he would prove entertain-
ing, but I had no idea what dangers lay ahead.

He told me of his god, the white Christ, who died but
lives again. I asked a lot of questions. He seemed to get irritated very quickly. Apparently his people usually keep their
questions to themselves. But Mama always said to ask questions. Better to ask than to forget. Be sure and you will not
get confused. This man, though, he expected me to be awed
by his big gold cross and his living-dead god. He told me his
staff could bring death to a man, and I laughed and said no
doubt it could. An axe can do the same, I added. He grew
pink then, insisting that it was the magic of his staff, not
the weight of it. His word for magic was 'blessed.' I found
that confusing. We blessed a house when it was built or a
bed when it was to hold a young couple. His blessing was
different—it was the power of his god, living in the staff. In
his hands too, he claimed. That made more sense. I did not
have it myself, but my auntie had possessed healing hands.
It was a good power but it did not pass to me. Still, he was
most odd in his opinions and I held my own counsel. No
need to disparage his beliefs.

But he pressed me to accept his god. I told him I had
gods enough, from Tapio's forests to Ilmatar's winds, right
on down to Akka's grain. He insisted though that I take up
his god, that I acknowledge his superiority. I demurred. My
gods built the world around me—what need had I of some

foreign god? Your god does not even speak my tongue, I
told him. Somewhat crossly, I admit. He grew angry then.
He cursed my stubbornness and my soup equally. I did not
mind the cries against the obstinacy of my heart, but I knew
my bread soup to be superb, flavored by the dried herbs
hung all over the cabin to dry throughout the year. Even a
man with burnt lips would know my soup was divine. This
man had no taste. Or else he was equally stubborn in his
heart.

I could have just said yes, pretended. It would have cost
nothing. But as I have said, I am pig-headed. I argued. I
reasoned. And perhaps worst of all for this man, I laughed.
I realize now that was my mistake. It was the beginning.
It was the first cold wind that means winter has come. He
struck me with his blessed stick. The first blow was unexpected. After that I curled up and ducked. He got so angry
so quickly, I could hardly believe it. Even my own father
did not lose his temper with such speed. His face grew red
as he chased me under the table with his stick and I was
overcome by giggling fits, as the scene reminded me so
much of childhood escapades, ducking under the table to
escape punishment for tasting the cakes before they cooled,
for neglecting chores, for speaking out of turn. My mirth-
ful outbreak infuriated him further and he sought in vain a
better chance to rain blows upon me. I was thankful in my
heart for the big birch table Lalli made for me when first I
came to him as a bride from my poor family, even as I could
not halt my laughter in its shelter.

But then as I paused, breathless and giddy, he got in a
good blow. The mighty hardwood struck my brow with a
loud crack, and a blinding white light filled my head. It was
the power of his god, I felt at once, filling my head with his
fury. I could see nothing as the hot sun grew in my eyes and
the voice of his god filled my head, swearing how I would
suffer and pay for my obstinacy. And like clouds moving
away in a storm wind, the light parted and it was as if I flew
on the raven's back into time rather than the sky, seeing
the new life unfold under this white god, a world of bright
light and dark shadows; worse, a world where my arts were
not needed, my wisdom was lost, and all the recipes Mama
made me memorize were gone and forgotten. This I saw as I

lay on the floor, half under my own table, feeling the lump grow on my forehead. I looked up at this new magic man and, to his credit, he looked somewhat aghast at what he had done.

It took some effort, I had to struggle up on one elbow, wave away his hand, and steady myself with the table's leg, but I stood on shaky legs, looked him in the eye, and spat.

He was unprepared. I think he was so certain the image of his white god would cow me that he could not imagine any defiance. He did not know us. Coming from his far away land, he did not understand what it takes to live here, to dig through the earth, to cast deep nets, to survive the winter's dark. He did not know my own family's cavernous willfulness. He does now. Wherever his spirit dwells, he knows now.

And so he left. Jammed his hat on his head, threw some coins on the floor and went out to prepare his sledge to depart, angrily strapping his horse back in, muttering all the while. I picked up his shiny gold from the floor, knowing what it meant for us, how Lalli's eyes would open wide and he would smile and rub his hands eagerly thinking of the cattle we could buy. Yet I could not accept it. I stepped outside, still wincing from the blow to my head, wiping away the sticky blood, and I threw the coins after his departing back, striking him and calling forth a string of curses.

When Lalli returned and saw the purplish knot under the poultice I had held to it for hours, he said nothing but grabbed his hand axe and set out at once across the icy lake in the tracks of the sledge. The axe was small, hardly a weapon. I did not think he would do any harm; at most he might threaten the man. But I did not understand how this white god worked, that death is a transformation. And this Henrik, he wanted that transformation. He got it.

Lalli returned, bloodied and stunned at his own change. He was embarrassed by his love for me which had propelled him to pursue the stranger across the ice and rain blows upon him. He sat at the table, a sullen look of pride on his face and the red hat upon his head, the occasional boast breaking the silence. It was only later that we realized the magic in that object, when at last he tired of the show, snatched the hat off, and howled with shock and pain. The ring, too, took his flesh off as he slipped it over his knuckle, leaving him almost too frightened to scream. Strong magic, vengeful conjuring.

It's no good, I conclude at last. I cannot fight such magics. My paltry store of cures and charms cannot kill, cannot fight a ghost. We will simply have to endure, as we always do. We will have to endure the mice, the anger of this ghost and his white god. We can do it. I will reach down into the black depths of my resistance and find my most gloomy persistence, and remain. We can both—

Suddenly the chills run like hunting dogs up my spine, as if my body senses before my thoughts do the danger here. Lalli's cry freezes me upon my stool by the fire. But as he continues to shout, I jump up at last and run to the door. I cannot believe it, even after all that has happened, I cannot trust my sight. My stomach rises, crimps, and struggles as my eyes take in the scene.

There must be thousands now. The tiny mice cover the ground and every bit of skin and cloth they can cling to, even as he bats them away, cursing and crying. I can only gape as he passes, picking up speed, heading for the old tree on the lake's edge. He will try to climb it; perhaps the mice will fall into the soft ice and water where the spring feeds the lake. Perhaps he can shake them off. He climbs up the lowest limb, stretching out over the ice, the tree swaying with his weight, and at last I begin to run, paying no attention to the biting wind, the throbbing in my head, thinking only of my Lalli, my Lalli. But I am too late, as I see the ice crack and open beneath the limb. It is not Vellamo's breath that rises from the floes, not Ahti's arm that stretches forth from the water. My heart sinks as I hear the limb echo the sound of the ice, a crisp snap, and still too far ahead of me I see Lalli tumble into the dark waters, many mice clinging yet, joining him in the depths. I have a mad thought of rescue, throwing a stout branch out to him, seeing him cling desperately to it and lugging his water-soaked body back to the shore. I could warm him by the fire, fill him with potent herbs and steaming soup, and he would not even get a fever. But I see the writhing white arm close about his struggling shape, and I know now that I must live with two ghosts.

Based on a murder ballad from the Kanteletar, 'Palakainen' gave me a chance to indulge in the gothic, for which I am always grateful. According to the edition of the ballad collection selected and translated by Keith Bosley, the title comes 'from Russian Pelagiya, but the Finnish name also has grisly overtones of pala(nen) 'titbit"(185) – brrr! It's a little too homey for the cannibalistic theme. I chose the mother's point of view because it gave a greater resonance to the tragedy of the girl who becomes a little titbit. I don't know where the tale's strange rhythmic prose came from, but it seemed to suit the story perfectly.

PALAKAINEN

HE CAME WITH RAVEN FEATHERS, OR SO IT SEEMED TO ME. HE CAME TO WOO OUR daughter. Had the wind whispered her secrets into his ear? For she would not have become the wife of any ordinary man, Kommi my husband made sure of that. Swanlike she was born, swanlike did she grow, with white hands and a graceful neck and eyes that looked unblinking at you. The servants, who all grumbled day and night about their work, would give her the best of the cream, the finest weaving, the sweetest *olut*. Her brothers and sisters too, who should have been jealous of the attention our little star received, instead protected her, coddled her. Her sisters did the mending rather than let her prick her fingers. Her brothers gathered kindling, which should be her job, carried hay to the cows in winter, rather than let her chap her hands. Swanlike they stayed, white.

The wind must have carried her sighs to the ears of Kojo's son. For all her gentle ways, for all her pampering, she dreamed as any child of growing up, of going away. No ordinary husband would be good enough. Kommi had sworn at her birth, when the white shock of hair made us all gasp, sworn that she would be protected, cosseted, loved. No fumbling farmboy would wed this child, no simple smithy get her hand. She was the sweet light of our hearth. And so it has always been, until now.

Kojonen did not send his son. The youth came of his own accord, much to his father's surprise. He had already set out on his own, put up his own farmstead, brought his cows to pasture, brewed his own *taari*. His father would have gladly shared his home, passed the keys to his fine son, passed the wealth. His son only smiled and declared that he needed his own household, required to see himself a man. And so alone, with only servants, his father kept a lonely home while his son toiled in new fields and ploughed up rough the earth, making his wealth even richer, making folks remark at market, 'Kojo's son is his own man. Wealth has not made him afraid to work.'

It seemed a good sign, when he came calling, seemed a faint squeak of hope that a worthy suitor had arrived. But Kommi would not make it easy, though he knew there was no other, though he thought that Kojo's son might well make a man worthy of his swan. She was no more keen to his offer, sat by the hearth and said not a word, though the slightest scarlet blushed climbed her lanky soft white neck when Kojo's son came a-calling, came to plead his lover's suit. But the wind, it must have heard her, when she often, in private, had sighed with longing true for a man who could keep her, guard her love and shelter her downy head.

So he came to our window, calling out to Kommi loud, 'Kommi, let me have your daughter! Swanlike, graceful—she's the one to brighten my poor homestead, to gently hold my tired head when the night is darkest and cold. Say you will give her to me!' There he was with hair as black and shiny as the raven's wing and eyes like hardened coal, and I felt a shiver go through me, like a piece of winter ice floating down the springtime river, come from the far north, from the distant lands of Pohjola. But I knew Kommi would not give her, not give up without a trial.

'I will give her, Kojo's son, only if you pass the trials, prove yourself worthy of our treasure, swanlike star of our own home.' Kommi's eyes were glowing with pleasure, with pride—but also with hope that this young corbie, this wealthy son, might be the one to pass the tests, to win the hand, to deserve the child of our hearts.

'Try me, Kommi, test my mettle. I will prove to be worthy of your prize.' A smile broke over his face, but did not reach his eyes. I should have known then, but I was blinded too, blinded by the wide white smile, by the thought of all that wealth, riches to shelter our little swan forever, to keep her hands so soft and fair.

Kommi leaned out from the window, rested his hands upon the sill. 'I will let you have my daughter if you can accomplish much. No simple farmer will win her hand, no laborer will take her home.'

'Challenge me, Kommi. For your beautiful swanlike

daughter, much will I prove. Any feat will I undertake to
have the white-winged beauty at my door.'

'Here's a task, mighty simple, any lad in knee pants
could fulfill it. You must shoot a star from heaven, any of
the twinkling lights between the shifting clouds. On one
foot must you complete this, with a single arrow at first try.'
Kommi smiled to relish the sight, seen only a time or two
before, the crestfallen suitor suitors with longing looks, cap
in hand, heading home.

But this *korppi* did not falter, fixed his cap down on his
head, slung his bow over his arm, and walked into the fields
to await nightfall. One by one the household folk gathered
to watch, some pretending they had work, or that the late
summer afternoon was perfect for small tasks of mending
and sewing. The brothers, the sisters gathered, curiosity
lighting their faces. Only she, our swan, our maiden, sat
alone by the fire, spinning wool, for she could not bear to
see what happened, could not stand to wait for night.

When at last the twilight gave way to evening's purple
hue, all who could were gathered there to await the test of
mettle, to try the lad of raven hair. Unconcerned, he gazed
at the star lights, as if to find the perfect one. All the pin-
points sparkled overhead like white pebbles in a pool. The
household joined together, looked upward to see the night
sky. When at last the time was right, when the black-haired
one had chosen, then he reared back on one leg, stretched
his bow until it curved like an ox yoke, until the tension
made his sinews strain, held it just one moment longer, then
released the fiery flame.

Upward shot the arrow, onward flew the dart. It was
decked with owl feathers, striped wings to aid its upward
flight. The point he had carved with care, hardened in the
crackling fire. Kojo's son watched the shot disappear, all
there craned their necks to see. But only black night met
our gazes, only darkness filled the sky. In time folks began to
chatter, wondering loudly how far up the smallest star, how
long must be the shot to reach that height. Kojo's son alone
stood silent, black eyes ever on the hollow darkness, his gaze
still patient, waiting. One by one the others gave up, went
to seek their soft feather beds. Kojo's son silent stood, still
on one foot, patient, waiting. Kommi and I stayed behind,

looking up at Ukko's night. How long passed, it was hard
to say. Kommi had just nodded off when I felt my breath
catch. I was uncertain at first, but then the twinkle grew.

It was the star. The brightness gained in size as it gained
in speed. Rousing Kommi, I sent him running to the house
to get the cooking pot, black as pitch. Stumbling, stumping
along close behind him came our servants, sleepy eyed and
rubbing faces, one foot still in a dream. All alone, by the
doorway, waited our girl, the swan-necked one.

From the sky, like a snowball, came the bright enchanted
star. In its center, we could soon see, was the arrow of Kojo's
son, owl feathers fluttering fast. Kommi placed the fateful
cauldron, found the most propitious spot. Like a downy
goose it landed, splashed down in the blackened bowl. We
gathered around it eagerly, our breaths held, our hands
shaking.

The star glimmered, but we could see it was fading. The
arrow pierced its very center. It lit our curious faces as we
gazed into the pot as into a prophetic pool. Something of its
celestial nature bathed our minds with hopes and dreams,
dazzled our wits with thoughts most high. But it glowed
a little less with each pulsating twinkle, and at long last,
accompanied by our sighs, the light went out and we were
once more in the dark. Nay, in the dawn; for the sun fore-
told its rising with a growing golden hue in the east. Kojo's
son stood on two feet and asked once more, 'Will you give
me your daughter now, the swanlike one to be my bride, to
set the kettle in my homestead, make the fire glow warm
and bright?'

Kommi gave one last look upon the cauldron black. 'You
have accomplished a great deed, but I will only give my
daughter if you can complete the next: Walk one day upon
knife points, walk another upon axe blades, both those days
upon the sharp points—prove the love you have for her.'
The eyes of Kojo's son glittered darkly in the dawn light, but
his white teeth flashed in the gloom. He said not a word,
but nodded slowly, turned and bent his steps for home.

We all took up the great cauldron, carried it upon poles
hoisted across strong backs. We let it cool the day and night,
and still the next morning the ember smoked. The arrow,
blackened by the flames, still stood upright in its heart.

Kommi at last gave a pull upon its darkened length, gingerly testing the temperature before grasping firmly. It turned to ashes in his hand, all but one singed owl feather, the rest just sooty charcoal dust. He took the heart of the dead star, wrapped it in a rough old cloth, gave it to his swan-like daughter sitting silent by the hearth. We all gaped at the dead star's center, at the lump of blackened coal. I will never know whether in its depths she saw the eyes of Kojo's dark-haired son.

People came from all the farmsteads, came to see the wonder dark. They gathered round in bright sunlight, or sought the hearth light in the shadows. None could say a greater wonder had been found in all this land than the star pierced by the arrow by the young man on one foot. Those who had seen the arched bow, seen the shot aimed for the sky, traded stories for good *olut* when abroad at market times. Silent in her accustomed corner, our daughter with her swanlike ways brooded on the star before her, but never spoke a word on it.

Kojo's son, the strongest of bowmen, spent his days out in the woods, gathering stumps of widest girth, yoking his bull to the roots. Weeks went by and still he gathered, chopping up the gnarly wood. High outside his new-built cookhouse he piled the wood of ancient trees. When the crisp fall leaves were turning, he turned at last to build the forge. He rolled a rock down from the mountains to give his blows a base, called upon a wizened servant to be the hands upon the bellows. From the farmstead of his father, he gathered all the bits of metal, rusty blades and pitted kettles left in dust and in neglect. All the pieces, all the iron went into the smithy's pot. Then the two men stoked the fire, got the flames a crackling red, orange tongues shooting forth.

From the forge, such a sound came a-ringing across the valley, over the mountain and to our home, ringing for the newly born smithy who had his grueling work to do. Long he pounded, long the fires blew, long the heat and hammers waved under the cooling sky. Talk arose across the valleys about the frenzied work of him who sought the swanlike maiden. Every tongue was wagging, offering opinions and local wisdom. But swanlike rested our daughter at the hearth, quiet with her simple tasks. Never a word she spoke.

Sometimes she gazed in silence at the charred heart of the
star, but she never offered her assessment, never had a word
to say.

At night in bed I would turn to Kommi, prod him to
made some kind of comment. 'What do you think he does
there? Will he come for our little one?' Kommi always
groaned and muttered, 'What will be, will come to be.'
I could say later that I knew, that my heart held some
tremulous whisper of what lay ahead, but all I had was a
foreboding, dark as the raven's smoky wing that brushes the
highest limbs of the forest when it glides in its hushed flight.

About the time of autumn harvest, when the nuts began
to fall, when the last wheat had been threshed and stored,
the hammer fell silent and every head turned. All the
months of gathering wood, of seeking out iron where it lay
fallow, all the weeks of pounding, pounding, until it seemed
Ilmarinen himself had taken up residence—ended one clear
and propitious day. And Kojo's son walked forth throughout
the valley in the crisp autumn air, calling on his friends and
neighbors, exhorting everyone who was there to bring forth
all their iron hatchets and every knife of every size. They
gathered all their sharpest points, brought them to the fields
of Kojo's son, to the furrows of the dark-haired one.

No crops grew upon his fields in the brittle autumn
morn, only well-honed blades of iron pointing ever heav-
enward. All the folk had gathered too, brought their biting
tips to pasture, stayed to see the feat of strength, the raven-
haired boy would no doubt carry out that day. No one else
would dare the tasks, no one else would even try to win the
swanlike beauty's hand. None but he would walk the field,
cross the cutting turf of iron. We too gathered there that
first day, Kommi standing at my side. All the brothers, all
the sisters, all left their chores behind. Alone the swanlike
daughter sat in silence by the hearth. She would not depart
our homestead, would not leave our warming fire.

The heavens shone down on Kojo's son who strode forth
on his new shoes. Weeks he had been forging these shoes,
hammering the iron to shape the toes. Now he stood before
us all, white teeth gleaming in the sun. He called us all to
witness, called on Kommi to repeat the challenge. One
day to walk upon knife points, another upon the blades of

hatchets. Iron yes, but thin and brittle—why did no one call it madness? Why did none speak out that day? Why did no one call it folly to win a swanlike maiden that way?

Coal-black were the eyes of that one as he trod upon the knives. Gasps were drawn and mumbling doubts poured forth—would the shoes withstand the blades? Kojo's son with sprightly mien crossed the new-sown field of points, turned and wandered back and forth as if it were a daily task. Admiration poured forth from mouths once grudging, more accustomed to finding fault. No one there from any village had anything but good to say about the *korppi*, Kojo's son, and his well-hewn smithing skills. Kommi watched with admiration and I could not stop myself from wondering almost aloud at the strength of those iron shoes that day. If the swanlike daughter had watched this, would she still sit silently by? Would she cheer to see the young man triumph in this mighty feat?

All the day he wandered back and forth over the hastily plowed field of knives. Across the valley the clang of metal rang out, an echo of his weeks of smithing by the glowing fire of the forge. Only when the red sun had slipped behind the mountain that divided his valley from ours, did he cease from his labors and step down from the sharpened blades. Then glad hands welcomed him there, passed him plenty of mugs of *taari* to speed recovery from that day. Many beheld the remarkable shoes, forged from every scrap of iron over the long pounding weeks past. Many marveled at the surface, mottled now with blade points' ire, felt the rough pocked surface, found it a suitable reward for his daylong toil. It was a quick decision to build a fire, a taste of celebration, but no fire burned as bright as the light in the eyes of Kojo's son. Kojonen himself was there, propped on his young son's arm. The dark of the night and the long day's deed dared by his raven-haired son seemed to leach all his strength away.

All night we sat by the fire. All night the folk celebrated the great deed and spoke well of the morrow. I could only think of my white-necked daughter, silent at home.

Came the morning and everyone stirred. All gathered to see the second day, the second task. Bleary-eyed they greeted the dawn, rubbing faces reddened by the bonfire's warmth.

Sprightly came the raven-haired one, eager for the new day's task. Once again his iron shoes were strapped on his feet, once again the local folk planted their sharp points, axes springing from the ground. Once again the field of iron stretched out across the valley and the clang of iron on iron rang out in the still autumn air. Back and forth across the blades, the dark son of Kojo strode. Hour after hour went by, accompanied only by the ringing echo and the furtive talk of neighbors.

It was a little past midday, when the sun had passed its zenith, that we heard the crack. We had become accustomed to the ringing rhythm of his steps, back and forth, crissing and crossing the field of axe blades in the weak autumn light. *Crack*—discordant across the valley, it grabbed our ears like an impatient mother, got our attention, brought us 'round. It was the weakness he could not hide, the flaw in his metal working.

He was no smith after all. He had surely done well, as well as he might with determination and hard work. But skill—had he asked, would any have known? Would Ilmarinen himself have been able to craft such shoes? Perhaps. The damage was done, the shoe was cracked, clanking as he stepped across the axe points, yet his stride slowed not one whit. All eyes were watchful, fixed upon the raven boy, as he continued on his journey. Grim-faced now he strode onward, eyes and shoes flashing bright. As the sun began to fall, still he limped across the blades. When at last the second crack rang out across the steel-plowed fields, even Kojo himself shook his head sadly, for surely the raven-haired one must yield. Too much to bear the sharp-edged garden, too much to bear the axes' points.

Kojo's son paused but a moment, then regained his halting steps. Though his pace was hampered now by two rough shoes that clanked and rang, on he went with determination, on his way toward the sundown. In silence we waited, our breaths as one, watching the red steps across the land. And not until the sun had dipped behind the hills did he stop.

All the mothers gathered near, crowded round the motherless boy. Not a word did he speak, not a tear fell from his eyes. But the red path of the day dried dark on the axe point

field. We could see the trail of rusty flecks leading back
and forth across the meadow. His eyes glittered. The task
had been accomplished, although a mighty price was paid.
Gentle hands reached for linen, murmuring mothers spread
their hands, ointments came from every corner, the cry went
out across the lands. But Kojo's son would not allow them,
would not let them seal and bind his wounds, until he had
addressed my Kommi, asked for the hand of the swanlike
one. He stood upon his painful wounds, looked my Kommi
in his eyes. 'Will you give me your daughter now, the swanlike one to be my bride, to set the kettle in my homestead,
make the fire glow warm and bright?'

Kommi gave one last look upon the field, axes sprouting
shiny, axes harvested and on their way home once more.
'You have accomplished a great deed, but I will only give my
daughter if you can complete the next: Swim the stagnant
pond of darkness, find the pike within its depths. Bring the
gold-finned one to our home, bright scales for the mother
of the bride. Only then will you have the snow bride, only
then the swanlike one.' Kojo's son nodded fiercely, turned
his back and strode away. Collapsed then her father upon
a wood chair, gave in to his weary thoughts. Murmuring
mothers soothed his bleeding, singing songs of iron's birth.
Kommi took my hand in his, turned our steps toward
home, while eager neighbors stoked the bonfire yet again.
At our hearth, the swanlike one bowed her head upon our
return, asked no questions, stirred the fire. Did she know
what lay ahead? Did she know the raven's heart?

The first soft dusting of winter's blanket fell the morn
that he set out, Kojo's son for the darkened pool, silent
now with furtive cold. Winter's calling card arrived and he
set out to swim the depths, to search the murky waters for
the golden pike. There were those who traveled with him,
those who bore the nets and carried the bucket of lard,
ready for the task. Kommi dressed and had his gruel, set out
for the banks with others, wore the elk fur round his ears.
I could not bring myself to leave the side of my swanlike
beauty young, part from her glowing ghostly hair. My heart
leapt to see her at the hearth, a hand reaching to stir the
kettle, the other with a needle poised. So I sank down on
the bench, took my share of daily mending. Silently our

needles bobbed in the failing daylight of the late year, under Ilmatar's frigid sighs, far from Näkki's cruel depths.

Try as I might to keep my mind as busy as my fingers, my eyes would stray repeatedly to the boiling surface of the kettle. In its tiny waves, I saw the lapping surface of the pool, saw our friends gathered on the bank as Kojo's son stripped himself. On the surface of the kettle, I saw the young man with raven hair smear his body with the lard, cover all the pale white flesh, protect it from the icy waters, sure to chill the corbie's skin. On the banks the older men stamped their feet, passed the bottle to and fro, blew on hands chapped with redness, then thrust them back into furry pockets. The young man with hair as black as night shivered on the gloomy shore, but he only paused a moment before leaping forward to plunge into the shadowy waves.

All this I saw in the kettle's darkness, all this I saw in our own snug home, the swanlike beauty at my side, my fated daughter on the bench. Her needle never faltered, and she never lost a stitch. Did she know, had she guessed, how her luck was thrown that day?

In the waters of the deep pool, Kojo's son dove through murky waves, kicking like a summer frog, twisting like a weasel swiftly through the depths, to the bottom where the pike lay in winter's silent waiting. Did I really see him wrestle with the golden shining one? Did I see him push off from the muddy bottom, one hand thrust in the gasping gills, the other grasping wide spread fins? Did I see the two rise, twisting, to the broken water's surface? Did I see the others, eager, gather up the fishing nets, spread the knotted fibers for the dark-haired son of Kojo? Did I see them wrap the wrestler in the rough wool blankets then?

Perhaps it was only in my mind's eye that I saw these wondrous things, but it was but a short time later that the young one came back here. Kommi did not meet my gaze when he came through the door with the raven one behind him, Kojo's son with heavy burden. On the table laid he the pike, the golden one still gasping his life out until at last he lay still. Not a word did they exchange, Kommi silent as the grave, Kojo's son with a grim smile. Kommi reached into the larder, brought forth a foaming mug to share. Sat beside

the black-haired young one, looked his age and something
more.

'Will you give me your daughter now, the swanlike one
to be my bride, to set the kettle in my homestead, make the
fire glow warm and bright?' His eyes glittered darkly, his
white teeth flashed between his lips.

Kommi sighed and looked toward me, where I sat yet by
the fire. My swanlike daughter never paused in her labors,
as the swift needle flew, but I had dropped my work in the
basket even as the visions grew. I could not cry out, 'No,
never! Never will you take our gentle daughter, take her
from our happy home,' for Kommi was already nodding,
hand out to the *korppi's* wing. 'You have won my swanlike
daughter for your own fireside. Keep her warm and keep
your kettle ever full of healthful food.'

The blush of blood grew on her cheek then, my rosy one
so near the fire. Knew she would be going soon, amid the
tears of family and friends, into the sleigh of the raven, into
the arms of Kojo's son. How many days was it we were still
with her? Hard to tell, so full of tasks—there was the bridal
gift to manage, all the linens she would need. Salted meats,
dried fruits, grain—all to make a larder full. Came the day,
all too swiftly, when the sleigh pulled up outside, took away
our swanlike beauty, took her from our family hearth. Tears
were shed by me, by sisters, even servants cried that day.
Empty was our home thereafter, as if the fire had been put
out, as if the baking lost its savor, as if the birch twigs lost
their scent.

I was in the sauna then, on the longest, darkest day when
the visions came again, showed me the fate of the snow-
white one. The *löyly* rose up, whispering softly, told a tale I
would not hear: How my lovely swanlike maiden rode with
the raven away from here. They had only crossed the river
when the wandering eye of my daughter saw the footprints
of a dog in the snow, running away from their trail. Kojo's
son grinned at her, nodded to the twisting track. 'Better far
if you were to follow little flop-ear's small footprints than
to follow Kojo's son.' My unequaled maiden said nothing
back, only drew the furs close about her, sank but lower in
the sleigh.

When they crossed through the far stand of birch trees,

just upon the small hill's rise, there the wolf's loping prints crossed the white expanse of snow. The *korppi* stretched his lips across his snow-white teeth, 'Better far if you were to follow the path of the lone wolf than to follow Kojo's son.' My lovely daughter, swanlike beauty, said nothing back, but drew the furs more tightly around her, shed no tear, but sank into the sleigh's shadowed depths.

They had climbed the final ridge, the cottage of Kojo's son in view, when the ambling tracks of the bear met their runner's path. The raven-headed one showed his teeth again, his black brows drawn together. 'Better far if you were to follow Otso's way, tread behind the honey-paw, than to meet your death in the raven's haven, in the home of Kojo's son.' My swan, my lovely one, shed a single trail of tears, but no sound did she make as the sleigh slipped ever faster down the ridge. The horse plunged along, his breath like smoke, as if he were on fire with some inexhaustible flame.

My own throat was less sanguine. I moaned aloud in pain and sank to the wooden floor. No *löyly* now; the vision receded, but I knew what I would have to do. I could not save my swanlike beauty, I could not save that special one, but knew I must go at once, to find the truth, to find the vision realized. I threw on my clothes and called for Matti, called for my oldest son—Kommi was away that day, in the woods, out a-hunting, or surely he would have shared the wild journey across the snow. Matti swiftly harnessed our old mare, while I wrapped myself in furs and climbed up on the creaking sleigh. Forward we raced, as fast as our poor mare could go. The snow fell harder and faster, the swirling white blocked my sight until further visions arrived, enchanted my sorrowful eyes.

There was Kojo's son reaching for the ancient warder hung on the wall in bitter times, yet still shining, sharp to bite. His Grandfather's sword he took from the high beam of the cottage, whispered to the war-time blade, 'Do you hunger for soft flesh? Do you dream of blood for spilling?' We both could feel the sabre's answer, that it dreamed of red hot blood, that it hungered for warm flesh. I could not cry out, make a sound, as Kojo's blade began its journey, whistled through the winter air, and bit the gentle skin of my swanlike one. One part for the swampland, one part for the raven, another for the wolf, and one more for the river; a final part, the worst of all, was left behind for me. The tender breasts of my lovely white-haired child, who would never nurse a child as I had nursed my special one, would never cradle her lover's head, cruelly made a gift for the mother of the swanlike one. Kojo's son, with homely skills, gentle kneading, careful measure, made for me a golden pie. No fish in this pie, but sweeter meat, flesh of my broken heart.

Matti urged on our true-born mare, and the cottage appeared too soon before us. I wanted to cry out, to stop the sleigh before we arrived, before the smoking chimney smiled, before the open door laughed. I could not wait until the sleigh came to a shuddering halt, but threw off my furs and leaped from the seat, could not stop my searching eyes. It was the wind that brought my tears, not the trail of vivid red. It was the smoke from the stone-set hearth that made the stinging water fall. It was not the crimson table, it was not the steaming pie, it was not the cruel mind that left the fork and mug for me, to taste the final piece of my sweet one, burn my mouth on golden crust.

No, it was the single lock of white hair, streaming from the kettle's rest, caught unwary in the battle, left behind to cheer my eye, to break my heart, to bring me relief. I caught it in my grieving hand, wrapped it round a mother's fingers, caressed my dear child one last time. The raven had flown, would never return either, skim the woods and darkened swamps alone. Three days, I knew, I would lay there crying, three days now until my death, three days to mourn the beauty of my gentle swanlike one. Never more would she return, never more to warm our hearth, farewell to our swanlike beauty, lost forever, now a part of field and stream, bird and mother, but no more seen.

This story tells of the training of a young shaman who doesn't quite know what she's in for. Finnish magic is all about knowledge—knowing histories and origins in particular. For more on Finnish magic, see Kati Koppana's book Snake Fat and Knotted Threads; *for more on northern Shamanism, read Ailo Gaup's book* The Shamanic Zone.

SINIKKA JOURNEYS NORTH

SINIKKA PAUSED AT THE EDGE OF THE CLEARING. A WIND WHISPERED THROUGH the birch trees that huddled protectively around the glade. At the center lay a rocky outcropping, flat enough to serve as a perch for the pitcher of water the young woman had carried with her. She set the jug down carefully and seated herself before it. She lay her hands upon the soft earth, fingers spread. Sinikka wasn't sure this would work, but she was desperate.

'Oh Maaemo, hear me, your poor child. My people starve without your help. Some envious *noita* has cast a curse upon us—our crops die, the forest creatures have fled. Even the spring has slowed to a trickle. Mother beneath our feet, Mother of grass, trees, rocks and clay—hear me, heed me. Take pity on us and share your abundance!' Sinikka tried to feel the heart of the ground with her fingertips. Maaemo must answer. Please, please, please.

A sudden breeze lifted the hair from the young woman's forehead, and she raised her eyes to see a sudden swirl of leaves rise from beyond the rocks. The wild motion did not dissipate, but rather grew stronger, faster, until Sinikka could see the vague outline of woman in the leaves. She felt a thrill of excitement—and fear. Now sticks and dust joined the leaves and the form became clearer, though the movement never ceased. It was hypnotic.

'What is your name, child?' The voice had the quiet resonance of an owl's, but the light touch of the cuckoo, too. It was both beautiful and fearsome.

'I am Sinikka, daughter of Laina, and I—'

'Why did you not send your *tietäjä*?'

Sinikka bowed her head. 'We no longer have a shaman. Old Matti and his boy were killed by a great mother bear. No one else had been brought up in the traditions. Forgive me, Mother, for being so bold, but my people are desperate.'

Maaemo's form swirled more slowly now, rustling softly. 'What is it you want, child?' she asked at last. 'Why do you beseech me?'

'Help us,' Sinikka begged, willing the tears to remain in her eyes and not pour forth. 'Onni works against us. Return his favor to us so we may share in your many blessings.'

Maaemo's leafy shape seemed to laugh. 'I do not control Fortune—Onni is free to travel as he wishes, as may all creatures who walk upon me. My bounty is free to all who wish to partake of it. I neither help nor harm anyone. I do not tell Tapio how to grow trees, nor Ahti how to wield the tides. I do not tell the rocks what they may do, nor the birds where they may fly, and I do not tell Onni whom to favor.'

'But, Maaemo—!' Sinikka caught herself. Not wise to use the goddess' true name before the goddess herself—especially when one is a foolish young woman with no experience in such things. Biting her lip, she began again. 'Dear Mother of us all, I ask pity. Pity for my people, starving and hopeless. We have no one to guide us or to speak to our wise ancestors. No one to charm the swift elk, to sing the fish into our nets, or to enchant our corn crops. We will perish, Great Mother!' Sinikka could not halt her tears now. Bitter and swift they poured forth through her fingers and splashed in small drops on the rock before her.

Maaemo sighed. 'What you need is a new *tietäjä*. Onni comes and goes—one can never rely on Fortune.' The goddess sighed again, and her ephemeral body twisted snake-like in the air, coiling and uncoiling, round and round.

It was mesmerizing, Sinikka realized, when at last she looked up. Wondrous, too, but now the emptiness of despair outweighed her awe. Without Onni her people would starve. This was her last hope. She did not want to leave the beautiful valley that had been her only home, but that was the plan her father and mother had argued with the elders. To leave, to abandon their homes. But this Sinikka could not bear. It would be an onerous journey to fight through the wilds, to risk crossing other people's hunting grounds. How far would they have to go? If Onni abandoned them, would any new homeland be any better? Sinikka could not rid herself of the image that had frightened her for weeks—

herself, alone, dying in the frozen North, the icy blasts mocking her. She shivered.

But she had a final tribute to offer to put off this fate. Though it would not alter the goddess's words, Sinikka must honor their meeting. 'I have brought water to cool your dry earth, Great Mother. Let me offer this sacrifice to you.' She poured the water from the pitcher upon the rock and watched the precious liquid run over the surface and seep into the grass surrounding it. She tried not to think of the dry fields around the village, the dust curls that followed everyone's footsteps, the brown husks of vegetation. Well, one jug of water could not do much anyway.

The whorl of leaves fell to the ground, and at once a rippling track, like a lemming's trail, arose on the earth and made a bee-line for the water. The goddess's immense power drove up the rock shelf, effortlessly lifting the boulders and juggling them one atop another. Sinikka's amazement did not keep her from jumping back, away from the grinding stones. She did not want to end up like meal between them. Maaemo laughed at the young girl's fear, but her words were kindly.

'It is kind of you to offer something so precious to me, child. I remember kindnesses. I cannot help you to capture Onni, but I know someone who might be willing to undertake such an inadvisable pursuit. Seek Louhi, in the North, in Pohjola. She is crafty but wise. Be very careful—and be kind. She has suffered much at the hands of mortals.'

Louhi! 'The elders say she is an evil sorceress,' Sinikka stuttered. 'Why would she help me?'

'Why indeed? It is a question you must ask of her.' Maaemo laughed. The stones wobbled, ready to fall.

Sinikka wailed. 'But how will I find her? I have never been out of this valley.'

'Keep your shadow to your left. At night follow the Great Bear. Do not stop until you reach her. Leave at once.' The rocks tumbled to earth like giant hail, crashing and rumbling across the ground.

Sinikka stood there with her mouth open. Leave now? Find Louhi? Follow the Great Bear? Don't stop until you reach her— Who? The Great Bear? Or Louhi? She trembled to think of meeting with either one. I could just go back to the village and say nothing, Sinikka told herself. And watch my mother starve, and my father burn with anger and disappointment—and feel my shame. She sighed. It would be so far, so cold. And only her pretty shawl covered the thin shift and three skirts—hardly enough to keep her warm. I will probably die before I have to worry about facing the powerful *noitakka*, Sinikka told herself glumly.

But she set off at once as Maaemo had instructed her. She kept her shadow always on her left and ate berries that she spied in the woods. When night fell Sinikka found where the Great Bear hung in the sky and kept her feet moving, though they had already grown more tired than she could ever remember them being, even last year dancing at Vappu to welcome the new green leaves. Then she had danced until the last embers died out and the next day paid the price as she carried out her chores. The village well-spring had seemed far indeed that day, and each step an agony. At least then the spring still ran freely, bubbling up over the rocks. Remembering everyone's despair as each day the trickle grew less, Sinikka lifted her tired feet more quickly, hurrying on to whatever lay ahead.

On the third day, toward sunset, she finally fell. Long before, the ground had become hard and cold, and this morning Sinikka had been dismayed to find herself trudging through snow. She sought to ignore the protesting of her feet and the numbness that was creeping along her legs. Just keep on, she told herself, you must, you must. Every step was higher than the last, as the hill grew sharply steeper. When at last it happened, Sinikka was on the ground before she knew she had fallen. Well, here is my dream, dying, alone in the frozen lands. My parents do not even know where I am, she thought dully. I cannot even cry, I am too tired, too thirsty. At least it is quicker than starving, Sinikka comforted herself. Let the snow come down and cover me. I am going to finally sleep.

But even as she resigned herself to her ill-luck, Sinikka heard a strange noise. Something was coming through the drifts, down the mountain, with a shambling gait and labored breath. An undeniable curiosity raised the young woman's eyes to see the approaching creature. Oh dear, thought Sinikka, my death is going to be even more horrible than I thought.

It was a bear.

It was an enormous she-bear who ambled slowly down the path, muttering to herself as if she had forgotten some important chore. Just kill me, Sinikka thought. One way or another I will end up in Tuonela. Let the black waters of Death close over my head now and bring me peace. She closed her eyes once more, laid her head down, and began trembling violently. It is only the cold, Sinikka assured her swiftly beating heart, even as the back of her neck grew hot.

After a time, when nothing happened, Sinikka opened her eyes again. She realized too that a strange sound filled her ears. With enormous effort, she lifted her head and turned it the other way. The bear had stopped to scratch herself on the rough outcropping of rock that hung over the path and she was evidently enjoying the biting surface, as her whuffling grunts attested. When at last her wriggling stopped, the bear dropped back down to her four footed-stance and sniffed at Sinikka. Her breath was warm and meaty.

'You come ill-prepared for the cold, skinless creature,' the bear said at last, rubbing her nose. 'You will perish. Soon.'

'I suppose so,' Sinikka agreed. Her fear had evaporated with the last of her body's warmth. She had become indifferent to the bear's hunger. It was rather peaceful.

'I know what you are. Your kind work in packs. Steal my sisters' and brothers' skins. Never ask. If you stayed where it was warm, you would not need them.' Sinikka could not even work up the energy to respond. She stared up at the bear and watched how the wind made patterns in her fur. The great bear stuck her nose right up to Sinikka's face and sniffed noisily. 'Why do you come here?'

Sinikka tried hard to remember. What did it matter anyway, her tired thoughts scolded, you are almost dead. I could not do it anyway; Maaemo was wrong. 'Maaemo.' The memories of the green forest, the warmth of it, flooded back. Sinikka smiled at the memory. My last visions will be warm.

'Maaemo sent you here?' The bear grumbled to herself for a few moments. 'What for?'

Sinikka strained to recall the reason, the name. In Maaemo's voice, it came to her: 'Louhi.' And it all returned: the meeting in the woods, the appeal, the disappointment—the fate of her village. 'Louhi, I need to find Louhi.'

The she-bear grumbled further irritation. 'I suppose Maaemo told you I would help you find her?'

With difficulty Sinikka answered. 'She just told me to go north, not stop, until I find...her.' Now maybe I can sleep, Sinikka thought warmly, closing her eyes again and laying her head back on the snow. Soon, soon, it will all be over. So she was quite unprepared for the sudden jerk at her neck, the choking sputtering of her throat rebelling as her body was dragged across the icy surface. 'What...?' But of course the bear's mouth was full and she could not respond to Sinikka's query. At last the cold cruel sensation stopped.

'Well, you'll have to get up on your own.'

Sinikka raised her head, fighting its urge to tremble with weakness. The bear was sitting upright, back against the rocks, paws on her hairy knees. Just like one of us, Sinikka thought.

'You'll die soon if I don't keep you warm. If Maaemo sent you, I suppose I must show kindness to one of her kin. But you have to come to me.' She opened her paws wide, like a welcoming mother—a mother with long black claws. 'Come, child. Before I lose all patience.'

Sinikka rolled onto her side, then pushed with one arm. She was not surprised to see that her fingers looked blue and pale. Her whole body shuddered as she tried to regain her feet, but somehow she stumbled—half walking, half falling—toward the great mother bear. At once Sinikka was enveloped in the earthy warmth, her head lolling with relief. She was asleep before the great head rested upon her own.

Sinikka awoke to the sensation of falling. She had no idea how long, how far, and feared that it would hurt a great deal when she hit the bottom at last. *If* she hit the bottom, Sinikka thought moments later, when her fall seemed no closer to its end. Perhaps the bear has thrown me down a crevice between mountains, she wondered with very little fear. How did I get here? The question did not concern her greatly. But she was looking for something...someone? Louhi.

And as the word entered her head, Sinikka found she was no longer falling but standing in a dark cave, its roof arching high over her head and several torches whipping their light around its broad expanse. And just as suddenly a figure was there before her: Louhi.

She had no claws, no sparks flew from her eyes, her skin was not scaly and green; yet at the sight of this old woman Sinikka felt terror flash through her body like the cold of the first swim in spring. Old woman! Was she even that? Human?

'I was human,' Louhi growled. Was she in my head, thought Sinikka. The voice was so clear. 'Humans showed me only hatred, crossed my magic, stole my daughter, my only treasure. Humans—and that damned rune-singer.' She turned away from Sinikka, fussing with some pots and grains as if the matter were already settled.

I must be wise, Sinikka, scolded herself. No time for anger. I need her help if I am to get back, get out, help my people. Again the urge to think about how she got here rose up, but Sinikka turned her jumbled thoughts to Louhi. She clasped her hands together (blue, blue hands, but no longer cold) and fell to her knees. 'Wise woman of the North, on my knees I beg you, please help me to save my village!'

Louhi turned, knife in one hand, pot in the other. 'And why should I do such a thing for some little wen like you? I have enough to keep me busy. Why should I take such a little bird under my wing?'

Sinikka thought hard. 'Your knowledge is so great. What a waste not to share it—'

'Ha!' The old woman's eyes flashed in the murky light. 'Always your people come, stealing my fire, stealing my gold, stealing my daughter. And what do I get in return? Hatred, tricks, lies!'

'I am but a poor young woman, great mother, trying to help my village keep from starving. I will offer you anything you want, if only you will share your great knowledge and teach me how to entice Onni. Our fate must change. Anything, anything I can give you.'

Louhi squinted at Sinikka shivering in the flickering darkness. 'Hmph. You come here in most unsuitable clothes—not a gold thread upon your hair, no silver strands upon your chest. No treasures, no staples even, no gifts. What do you have to give?'

Sinikka's head dropped. 'I have nothing. I came here because I have nothing, my people have nothing, and we are desperate. I asked Maaemo for help but she refused to help me catch Onni. But she did send me north to seek you. She said if anyone can capture Onni, it is you. You are so clever and learned—'

'Bah! Learned! I am simply old. Living long has been my learning, keeping my eyes open. I am no foolish wizard or rune-singer. I just know a thing or two.' She smiled at that and seemed to lose herself in thought. Sinikka thought it best not to interrupt her reverie. In time she continued. 'So you have nothing, and you come to me empty-handed, unskilled, unschooled, and unwanted. Ha! You are worse off than you know.'

Sinikka felt the sting of her words and her cheeks grew red as berries. But a spark of inspiration glimmered in her thoughts. Would it work? Oh, may my foremothers preserve me and give me courage! She took a deep breath. 'It is true I have nothing. I can offer only myself. You have lost a daughter. Let me be a daughter to you.'

The old wisewoman's hands froze in mid-air. In the sudden silence, Sinikka realized just how much noise the two of them made. There was only the whispering sputter of one of the candles as it went out. Time hung in the quiet. Louhi turned at last to stare at Sinikka, her hands on her hips now. Though it made her tremble, Sinikka looked into the eyes of the old sorceress, eyes the blue of a glacial river— just as cold, just as fierce. I am the cold, I am the snow, I am the ice, Sinikka told herself. I can face her fury.

Just then the old woman threw her head back—and laughed. She roared and shook with it, until she had to hold her stomach in pain. At first Sinikka could only gape at her in surprise, astonished by this unexpected outburst, but gradually she blushed red once more and became angry herself. 'You laugh at my offer. I know I am not much. I am not worthy. You might as well kill me now, before I become so angry I try to kill you!'

But her speech had only the effect of increasing Louhi's merriment. The old wisewoman finally sat down upon the floor and dried her tears with her apron, chuckling to herself all the while and rocking back and forth. 'Come, sit down beside me, daughter!' She beckoned to Sinikka, who reluctantly got up from her knees and walked over to Louhi and, after peering carefully at her face, sat down.

To her surprise, the old woman clasped Sinikka's hands in her own, forcing the girl to meet her eyes. But the blue that had been the color of stormy rivers now crinkled like waving cornflowers, and a smile lit the ancient face. 'You made me laugh, now there's a thing. I can't remember the last time. Now, now. Don't feel embarrassed again. You cannot know what a terrible life you offered yourself up for—your simple gift. Your immense sacrifice.' The smile had faded away, but her voice was gentle. 'What is your name, girl?'

'Sinikka.'

'Sinikka, you must be very, very careful to whom you offer the only thing you humans truly possess. Your spirit is not only the greatest gift, it is your only true value. All else fades.'

'But I only wanted—'

'Yes, yes, I know. To help your village, to save your people. Your generosity is admirable—but misplaced. You cannot deliver the ones you love from harm by giving up the only thing that will protect them: You.'

'Me?'

'Girl, your spirit is bold and fearless and will continue to grow. You are the source of power for your village. You need not look here for my aid. Trust your own strength. Trust your own thoughts. Don't wait for anyone to save you. You have the source within you.'

'But I know nothing,' Sinikka cried. 'I have never been out of our village, I can't ever weave cloth straight, and I've never even caught one fish that didn't slip away. I drop things all the time too,' she added, eyes downcast.

Louhi barked with quick laughter. 'You have spoken with Maaemo, traveled alone to the frozen north, survived a bear and,' she slapped her chest, 'the terrifying Louhi. Have you ever thought that you were not meant to weave cloth and catch fish and sow barley in the fields?'

Sinikka let an awkward smile creep across her mouth until it became a grin. Louhi let go her hands and clasped her shoulders warmly. 'Come! I have something to show you, a simple charm, but it will attract our friend Onni.'

'You mean it?!'

'It may attract him,' Louhi said, her face again stern. 'But you will need to persuade him to stay. He is greedy and fickle, he must be wooed. Now help me up, dear, my bones ache so today.'

Sinikka leaped up, pulled the old crone to her feet, and they turned to the table filled with pots and jars. The candles seemed to burn more brightly now, or perhaps her eyes had adjusted to the darkness. Sinikka watched carefully as the wisewoman concocted a pleasing variety of scents and textures: berries and herbs and nuts and roots, and even some kinds of dried fruits. She sang a runo that told the origin of the charm, detailing the ingredients. 'Remember them!' she admonished Sinikka with a wagging finger.

When Louhi was satisfied with the blend, she poured the contents into a small bag of soft leather. Tooled into the skin were ancient symbols which Louhi patiently explained one by one. 'This for the sun, and this one for the moon. Here is Maaemo, here Tapio. And here, this you can see is Ahti's river, there Ukko's thunder. And here, under all of them, me. I lie at the depths. Our names summon power. Use them carefully.' She handed the bag to Sinikka. It felt warm to her skin.

'Thank you, thank you so much, Louhi.' Sinikka felt the tears ready and blinked them away. She knew this small bag held the salvation of her people.

But the old woman waved her gratitude away. 'You should be going. You still have a long way back.'

Another inspiration seized the young woman. 'Come back with me. My people will sing your praises, we will honor you, we will celebrate your wisdom.'

Louhi laughed. 'They will run from me, they will cower in fear, they will curse my name. I am not fit to be seen by just anyone, girl. And not many are fit to be seen by me. But you are kind. No, I will ask though, that you come back and see me from time to time, to share my dark world for a time. But now, you must go. Stand here, upon this rock, here. Arms crossed, there. Now, close your eyes. Take care. Good-bye!'

And before Sinikka could echo the farewell, she felt herself hurtling upward, faster and faster, as the world outside her closed eyes became brighter and brighter. The wind whistled in her ears like shrill winter's blast until it seemed almost too much and suddenly she stopped. Sinikka opened her eyes and she was back in the snow by the rock, but this time she felt warm and awake and alive.

Sinikka sensed a weight upon her body and turning her head, she saw a great bear cloak wrapped around her shoulders. Her mouth flew open. She jumped to her feet and held the huge paws out. It was huge. For a time Sinikka could only marvel at the beauty of it. Then she wrapped herself once more in its warmth, threw back her head and cried out, 'Thank you, Great Mother Bear! This gift I will honor for the rest of my life. I will remember how you protected me on my journey and kept me warm. Your kindness will be praised forever.' And Sinikka turned back the way she had come, her shadow on her right this time, and ran through the snow down the mountain side. The runo for the Onni charm came to her mind, and Sinikka sang the secret words aloud as she hopped from one frozen rock to the next.

Sinikka had nearly reached the valley again when a swirl of leaves rose up before her. The young woman was tired but still oddly joyful, and the sudden appearance of Maaemo was a welcome one. She knelt to touch the earth, calling out, 'Greetings, Mother! All blessings upon you and your abundance.'

'You look happy, child. I take it your journey has been fruitful—and that you found the Great Bear as well,' Maaemo said, as the winds lifted an eddy of leaves, twigs and stones.

Sinikka smiled and patted the cloak slung over her shoulder. 'Thank you for sending me forth. I have learned much, and,' she added, holding up the small leather bag, 'Louhi has shared her knowledge with me. This will return fortune to my village, she has promised.'

A chuckle swelled from within the debris. 'Louhi's help often has costs. Be prepared. Still, I am glad you found what you were seeking.'

'Louhi was frightening—at first. She is a difficult teacher, but a wise one. It is a beginning. But Louhi told me that we must woo Onni if he is to remain with us. I am not entirely sure how we will do so. My people still have no *tietäjä*.'

'Oh, yes. Yes, they do.' The laughter this time was full and echoed all around the young woman where she knelt. When at last it died away, Sinikka stood, smiled, and walked back to her village, her spirits soaring higher with each swinging step.

Modern Dreams

'Vironsusi' is the Finnish word for 'werewolf,' although it also refers to Estonians, who may have been blamed for creating the strange creatures. In researching Finnish werewolf tales, I discovered that people rescued from that fate often retained their tails. What if that wasn't all that remained?

Vironsusi

Running, running, paws dragging from fatigue, and still the hunt calls across the hills. The bark of the pack urges me on and I dare not stop, dare not let them sniff me too long and find I am not *truly* one of them. Our quarry is rabbit—long strides, hopping desperately across the November snow, little scoops of white kicked up in its trail. It wouldn't be a great meal, not for a pack anyway. But the fun of it, the invigorating thrill of the run, the chase, intoxicates us all as we run, tongues lolling, breath coming in harsh pants. I bend low, reaching my jaws toward the scurrying prey, but then I hear it once again from far behind me: 'Taru, Taru.' The sound of my mother's voice calling my name breaks the spell and suddenly I'm running on human feet, and the pack quickly leaves me far behind without so much as a parting growl. The sob that bursts from my chest rips me from my nightly dream and I lie silently, hoping I have not awakened my mother beside me.

In the crisp cold of the dawn I rise and stir the fire. A few sticks soon have the blaze crepitating, and I put the kettle on for mother's coffee. Bundling up for the cold blast of February, I step outside and trudge toward the barn where the cows already murmur their complaint. I hide my tail under three skirts, but still they do not trust me. As I sit milking at the oldest one, a bossy brindle with overlong teats, I can feel her barely contained fear. They have become used to me, but they do not like me; I will always seem a predator to them. The cows reassure one another with long bellowing moos when at last I let them out and carry the milk back to the house. They are fearful, relieved to have escaped death at my hands once again.

Mother is up, warming her crippled hands over the fire as she stirs the porridge and sips her mug of coffee. I offer her milk to sweeten the inky blackness, but she waves it away. A mug awaits me, and I try to limit the milk I pour into it. It is still difficult for me to stomach the bitter fluid, but it makes Mother happy to see me drink coffee. It is a normal thing to do.

Together we eat our porridge wordlessly. I long ago gave up trying to come up with topics of conversation. It is still an effort for me, and there is little we can share. She does not want to hear that the crows still taunt me whenever I go to the woodpile, or that I can smell the first thaw to be only days away, though it will not last for long. Anything that reminds her of my shame brings the furrows to her forehead and the frown to her lips. When that happens, I lower my gaze like a dutiful daughter, although I am not ashamed.

Today is the day I have awaited for a very long time. Today Mother accompanies the Koskinens to town in their old Ford auto, to go to the market and to buy more hymnals for the church. Mother has *tutt*ed and reconsidered a dozen times or more; but as of yesterday, she could not reconcile staying home. It would provoke talk if she were to admit why, and Mother does not like there to be talk. It is difficult enough for a widow to live virtuously even with her daughter as her only company. Mother was able to conceal my initial absence because it was winter and illness abounded throughout the district. My continued weakness keeps me from traveling with them, she will explain, but I can wave from the doorway, my long skirts never leaving the floor. It will be safe enough.

Mother looks up as if she can sense my thoughts. I try to smile reassuringly, but I cannot seem to manage to keep it from looking like a grimace. 'It will be all right,' I say, startled yet again at the sound of my human voice. She shrugs and continues to spoon the sticky porridge into her mouth, chewing as contemplatively as the cows in the barn. I finish my coffee, swallowing the last mouthful with a barely concealed disgust, and take my bowl and mug over to the washtub. As I work the handle of the pump, I glance out the small window. A pair of jays argues in the copse of birches, their cries audible through the thin glass pane. I let my gaze follow them into the forest and blink as I glimpse a blur of grey fur in the distance. Is it my imagination? Is it just the product of my desire? I narrow my human eyes, but they are not up to the task. If there had been anything there, it was gone now.

I turn to see Mother staring at me. There is no accusation in her look, but I feel resentment rising in my breast nonetheless. I quash it and reach for her dishes. Let me be helpful, the gesture says; I am human after all, we are human together. Her eyes flick to the window and see nothing to alarm. Even the jays have disappeared. I put my head down over the tub and wash the dishes carefully. The ceramic mugs feel fragile and slippery in my fingers. The water, too cold, numbs my digits, but I focus all my attention upon the task and comfort returns to my jangling mind for a time.

Together we sweep the floors and wash the windows while the dough rises near the hearth. It is still early, but Mother insists we sit together for a few minutes before the Koskinens arrive so she can read Bible verses to me. I comply in silence, but the words chatter past my ears like the calls of birds I do not know. For her, the Bible was the key that saved me from sin and perdition. It was the good magic that broke the black spell around me. If I had not been so foolish, if I had not retained my good red scarf, she would not have known that the smallest wolf of the pack was I. She would not have called my name, broke the spell. Perhaps she suspects my secret desires. After all, in her eyes my tail remains not because the magic was insufficient, but because I was to blame and must pay for my crimes and the wildness in my heart. I know it is Mother's hope that the daily lessons will restore my soul to cleanliness. I feel a twitch in my tail where it curls beside my leg. Sitting in a chair has become so uncomfortable for me that I do not think I could long concentrate even if I did find comfort in her book. When she closes the covers with a gentle snap, I keep my eyes upon the floor in a pallid picture of penance.

'You will be safe at home.' Undeniably, there is a question in her statement which teases my ears, asking me to try to deny it. Instead I ignore it. She moves to the door. Her bundle of wares sits at the ready, and she leans her head to hear the murmur of the Ford approaching. Absently, I arrange my skirts around me. It is the first time I will have seen others since my return, the first time it has been allowed. Mother looks over her shoulder at me, worried, but I try to reassure her with my bared teeth. It is as much like a smile as I can manage with the distracting thought of freedom occupying the space between my ears. The purr of the auto's motor is louder now, and as she opens the door I can see the sickly green of its hide coming up the path, the color a mocking retort to the brown leaves and bare tree trunks surrounding it.

Mother looks back at me once more as she picks up the bundle. A single whispered word: 'Stay.' As if I were a dog, as if I were a tame thing. She ought to know better, but I simply nod and let her pass outside. Dutifully, I wave my hand to the Koskinens, careful to keep my distance, not rising up on my toes as one tends to do. No good letting the tail show after this careful charade. The old couple return the gesture with energetic good will, happy to see me recovering so well from my long illness. The pink of my cheeks offers a good simulacrum of health and wellness. The breath in my lungs becomes shallow as I watch the auto retreat from our gate, and a small whine escapes when at last it disappears from sight.

I do wait. They could turn back. Mother may invent a pretext to return, to check on me and be sure that I am safe, inside. So I linger, standing yet in the doorway, nose to the shifting winds. When I am certain that the car will not turn back, that I do not hear the hum of its motor any more, I step away from the door, closing it behind me. The sound of the latch clicking home makes me bark with laughter.

While I cannot resist looking back once more toward the path where the rumbling motorcar disappeared, I know I am safe now. I run across the yard to the sauna. Stepping inside I undress swiftly, folding my clothes neatly to lay them on the bench. It is such a relief to remove the three heavy skirts. Mother cannot bear to see my tail. She turns aside when I crawl in bed with only my shift for cover. Now I stand naked, my brushy tail waving gently in the closeness of the wooden walls. The bucket is already filled and I thrust my face into the cold surface, yelping with the shock of it, but glorying in its bite.

I go to the door and peer through the small crack of light. All around is silence but for the lowing of the cows and the chirping of the birds. It is broad daylight now, but there will be no one near. They will all be busy at tasks close to home: mending harnesses, knitting sweaters, kneading bread. It's too close to the dark time for there to be much in the way of hunting, and the grouse have become shy and scarce this late. Yet I hesitate.

But the urge proves too strong to resist for long. I slip through the door and trot across the clearing and duck into the woods. Even in the bright sunlight the chill stings like a slap, and I pick up the pace to warm this pink skin. The lingering patches of snow snap at my feet, but I run on heedlessly, wishing I were on four feet instead of two. I stop at the rise between the pines and turn back toward the farm. The house looks very small from here.

I crouch down, nose in the air. My sense of smell remains keen in my two-legged form, if less than it had been. I catch the scent of a rabbit nearby and charge into the brush to flush it. Startled, it leaps wildly, big feet flapping behind its escape. I give chase although my human legs are no match for the rabbit's speed. The thrill of the pursuit is enough to pink my cheeks and draw in great lungfuls of the crisp air. As I bend under the low branches of a young birch though, I pull up short. I did not expect to see one of my own pack standing there.

He's there, staring at me in something approaching disbelief, his tail moving almost imperceptibly behind him. I feel a surge of excitement. The wind ruffles his fur. But something in his eye holds me back. I know I look different, but don't I smell the same as I had then? I wave my tail gently back and forth, waiting. His nose dips up and down. His confusion distresses me, but there is nothing I can do. I feel a whimper escape my lips. I stoop and rest my fingers on the ground. Perhaps a crouch seems less alien. He shakes his head and lets out that bark I know so well, that sounds more like a groan in its wistful whine.

The old one recognizes me, but he doesn't like the way I look. I whine again, raising my own nose high and lowering my tail as much as possible. I cannot bring it all the way under my belly as I used to do. My human anatomy is not designed to work with a tail. Nonetheless, he steps forward, curious but not entirely welcoming. His tail raises level with his back, so I remain where I am, meeting his eyes and then

glancing away. He stalks toward me a little stiffly, still cau-
tious. His nose bobs before him as he approaches. I yearn
for the feel of his cheek against mine and close my eyes in
anticipation.

It seems like a lifetime, however, before the soft touch of
his hairy cheek greets mine. There's just the briefest brush
before he moves on, sniffing my pink skin suspiciously. I
remain immobile in my crouch and enjoy the tickle of his
whiskers along my side. He sniffs at my tail, puzzled, then
continues the circuit around me. He groans at my other
cheek, but his tone is more playful this time. I respond with
a whine and rub my cheek against his. He barks sharply but
does not move away.

If I were a wolf still, we could run away into the forest
and I would never have to look back. With a rush of yearn-
ing, I lay my head upon his back, but he jerks away, head
tilted. I have moved too quickly, I know. I am still not right
in his eyes, his nose. But my need compels me. I whimper
a little and rub my shoulder against his. He gives me a low
growl but does not move away. I try again, laying my head
on the top of his bony spine, as if we were lovers, as if we
were mates, but he turns to snap at me and I yelp, startled.
He does not move away, but he lifts his lip in a snarl, tail
raised high. At last I understand. It's no good.

I am not a wolf. Not really.

I feel a howl well up from my throat. He is kind enough
to reach his muzzle to the sky and join my dirge. But I know
what our shared lamentation means: good-bye. He sniffs my
nose and lays his cheek aside mine once more. The grizzled
grey around his jaws makes my heart ache. Tears blur my
vision. I look sideways at him, his eye closest to mine open
and frank. He nips my shoulder gently and gives a small
groaning bark.

And then he's gone, trotting off between the trunks
without another backward glance. The cry in my throat is
human now, and I weep loudly as he picks up speed. I think
back and I wish again a thousand times that my mother had
not called my name, that she had not figured out it was me,
the wolf with the red scarf. I had tried, those first few weeks
back on two legs, to find a spell, to find the way to return;
but I was incomplete, insufficient. Nothing worked. My

sobs echo across the forest, stilling for a moment the buntings' cries. The tears on my cheek sting with cold. The wind no longer feels brisk and invigorating, but biting and harsh. My tail droops to brush the ground.

I crawl under the limbs of an ancient pine, curling into a ball and wrapping my tail around me. There is nothing to do but wait for the chill to come and cover me like a quilt. The bunting calls to his mate again, comforting her, and reminding me that I am alone.

Runo 17 of the Kalevala *tells the tale of the giant Antero Vipunen, who has extensive knowledge of magic and charms, but who falls asleep and becomes a mountain after a long time. I had fun imagining an impatient modern hiker running into the stuff of legends, inadvertently joining the venerable sage Väinämöinen in his mythic journey to obtain Vipunen's secrets.*

Vipunen

'Well, quite a way to meet!' the old man said warmly, as if for the first time, but I could only glare at him. How long had we been down here? At least, how long had I been down here—he could have been here for centuries for all I knew. It felt like days for me, but looking at my watch—if the time was still right, who knew with all these strange things going on—it appeared as if it were half past four. But was that day or night? And why did that pool smell like something gangrenous had recently choked out its life in the black waters?

In the cavern my exhalation of disgust and annoyance echoed on for long after I had shut my mouth, the quiet susurrations crawling away from me like escaping mice. It was a very creepy moment. I looked over at the old man who seemed, at first, to have nodded off. I studied his clothes. They were not from this decade. To be charitable, they were not from this century—unless he was one of those re-enactor types or perhaps a folk-dancer. Well, that seemed more likely an explanation for the red skull cap, the wooly tunic and the cross-tied leggings. Was he actually wearing birch bark shoes?! Heavens. Well, that would have to be folk dancing. I don't think anyone's re-enacting the *Kalevala*, unless the folk movement here in Finland has taken a new and horrifying turn.

Presently I noticed his eyes were not entirely closed and, in fact, there seemed to be a bit of twinkle in them. I had just got to the point where I was contemplating his beard, thinking to myself, my gods, how many years has that thing grown? How many days of missed shaving, I thought as I rubbed my own clean-shaven chin. Formerly clean-shaven, I should say, for I was shocked to find that my whiskers had grown more than a day's length (and I am not heavily bearded, something to do with my fair hair, I suppose), and the realization of just how long I must have been down this

hole suddenly came to mind. It must be that shabby growth
which tickled the old man so.

'I was born with this beard,' he said, patting it proudly
as if it were some kind of treasure. 'A few more years down
here, you could have a splendid start on one...'

I squelched the sudden sense of panic and cleared my
throat to show I was not afraid. 'I have no intention of being
down here that long, old man. I was just resting and...diso-
riented.' I stood up decisively and put my fists on my hips.
'You may care to rot down here, old man, but I intend to do
something about it!'

'I have a name, you know,' he said mildly. 'I'd be glad to
tell you what it is, if you have any curiosity—not that I'm
assuming!' He smiled with half his mouth.

I was not about to cave in this easily. 'I notice you did
not ask mine.'

'Ah, but I know yours already.'

I did not let him see that this upset me. Ever so casually, I
turned and folded my arms as if I had very important things
to do. Which I did, if I was going to get out of here. 'Do
you, then? Well, that's practically magical, old man.' I'm
sure he could feel the subtle emphasis I put on those last
two words, but perhaps not—he might well be hard of hearing. 'So, what's my name then?'

'Eino.' He was clever. He didn't even look smug.

'Hmmph. Well, I suppose I am to be impressed by that.'
I was not about to believe that there was anything the least
bit odd about this old man or this place or the seemingly
elastic sense of time that was beginning to settle upon us.
Even if he had guessed my name correctly somehow.

He shrugged. 'You need not be impressed.'

I was silent. This old goat was not going to make me ask
how he knew my name. I would travel to the ends of the
earth before I would condescend to ask. Ends of the earth!
Perhaps I was already there; this god-forsaken gap could
well be the lowest point attainable from the upper crust of
the planet. And it was all a bit vague how I had come here.
I tenderly touched my forehead. Maybe this bump on my
head would remind me in time.

'It's on your backpack,' the old man said quietly. Perhaps
he was afraid of my reaction. I could feel my cheeks burn

crimson, but in the mottled darkness, he would be unlikely to see that. Still, it irritated me to know he was laughing inside at me.

'Eino Lahtinen,' he said, pointing at the label written in indelible ink. Of course; I had not been surprised, not really. It was perfectly logical after all. 'Well then, so—are you going to tell me your name?'

'Väinö.' He smiled as if I had probably already guessed it myself. I'm sure he had meant to appear kindly, but how insufferably haughty he seemed right then. I bet his real name was just Matti or Hannu. Väinö, indeed! Perhaps I should ask him to chant a few rune songs.

'Well, then, I'm sure you can charm us out of here in no time, eh, old magician?' Let him have a taste of his own medicine. I'm not without a sense of humor myself.

He shook his head, though, and smiled. 'Not until I get what I came for.'

Impossible, this man! Obviously waiting for me to do the difficult work. Well, I am in pretty good shape, all this hiking on my weekends and summers. That's right! I was hiking when I fell through the entrance to this cavern! How could I forget that? It seemed clear all at once—although there was that odd sense of falling ever so slowly, as if time had begun to stretch even then. Well, that was no more than to be expected. Too much television! And films. We get used to seeing tragic events unfold in painful slow-motion, and we impose such impressions upon our own experiences. Sad really, that our imaginations have been atrophied by the media. I should write a paper on that when I get back.

I turned back to the old man, rubbing my hands together industriously. 'So, old Väinö, what were you doing, looking for some toadstools for your soup?' I asked cheerily. 'Maybe some cave-dwelling marshmallow root? Well, let's find them and then be on our way. There seems to be enough brush and small bushes to grab hold of and help us make our way back up top. Pity we don't have a rope, but then I hadn't expected to be mountain climbing.'

Old greybeard smiled but shook his head. 'I don't expect that we will simply climb out of here. Vipunen won't allow such an easy climb. We shall have to be much more clever than that.'

'Vipunen? Is that what this cave is called, hmmm. I don't recall seeing it marked on my hiking guide. I came by way of Sword Point Ridge and had just passed over Battle Axe, when I fell.'

Väinö nodded. 'And you started at Young Woman's Needle?' He chuckled, half to himself it seemed.

'Yes, actually that was the route I took. Fairly common, I suppose. I'm sure a lot of people follow that route. After all the rating is 'difficult' but the elevation isn't all that much. I figured it would be a good challenge for the weekend.' And how many days had I been here now? If I were missing Huhtala's Business Ethics…! I hope Anikka was taking notes for me; she couldn't be bothered to come along. Well, now I shouldn't think that—poor dear! What if she had been stuck down here too? I would certainly feel bad about that.

'It's a rather unusual route,' the old one mused. 'You need special shoes.' He showed me his ridiculous shoes, taking them off and pointing to the steel inside the birch bark. I guess that would give support, although they looked wickedly uncomfortable. I had my Vasque Ibex, which had been quite an investment, I can tell you. He looked them over and nodded, as if they too met his satisfaction. For one hundred and seventy Euros I certainly hoped they would measure up.

'I had charmed a boat of curly birch wood from my knife, but the water leads nowhere useful,' he confided to me then, as if the shoes have given us some kind of bond. Great, not only old but delusional. Not that I would get in that water. It was the only thing you could smell down here, apart from the acrid dirt of the cavern's floor. The briny shine of its opaque surface would be enough to keep me out. Yet old Väinö said he not only sailed across it, but did so in a boat he conjured with his curly birch-handled knife. And I am the Crown Prince of New Zealand.

He patted his knife at his belt. Trusty old knife—now, there's something to worry about: Crazy old man who's armed. Well, surely he cannot move all that fast. I would be more than a match for the like of him, I could see that. After all, I keep to a regular schedule of workouts and hiking. I am quite fit, unlike some of my cohorts who never seem to make it outside the computer lab or the library. And besides,

I do have my own Swiss Army knife. No disadvantage at all between us then.

'We should start a fire,' he said. Sensible enough—it would give us a little more light to see by as well be warming in this drafty chamber. I'm not sure why we had still been just sitting in the gloomy darkness squinting at one another for endless hours—or, ye gods, days? Must have been the bump on my head. Now, did I get that on the way down? Surely, as I fell I had bumped up against something, rocks, or whatever. Although the rest of the ground felt soft and rather moist, there were small bushes and rocks scattered around.

We set ourselves to the task of gathering wood. Most of it was very damp—rivulets seemed to trickle everywhere—but in ten minutes or so we had a reasonable pile of fuel. The old rune singer, as I amused myself to think of him now, drew together the smallest branches and began laboriously striking a flint. I stared impatiently at him for a time and finally sighed, grabbed my backpack, and zipped open the side pocket.

'Here,' I tossed him my waterproof box of matches. He caught them nimbly but then stared dumbly at the box, as if he had trouble reading the instructions. 'Let me,' I said, thinking we could be here another hundred years otherwise. I pulled out a stick and struck it, holding the flame as close to the little pile as possible. I was ready to smack the old guy when he tried to blow on the flame, but fortunately it didn't go out but rather caught the kindling, which began to burn with a smoky belch. That was definitely more cheery.

Until I looked around us.

There was never a cave like this in my memory. The walls seeped, not so unusual in itself, but the smell was more foul than anything in my memory, and the gelatinous gleam they gave off was distinctly uncommon. Water could do odd things—given a century or several—yet this cave's sides looked like heavy folds of meat, fleshy and rotting. No pleasant oxide hues here, but a blend of veal-red ochre and ripe liver-brown. I shuddered. The flickering tongues of the fire gave a leaping light to the cavern, making it seem almost undulating with life.

'Well, now,' I said, trying to maintain a look of confidence. 'What shall we do now? Shall we make for the source of the light up there? We can make torches of the larger branches once they get going. They won't give much light, but some is better than—'

'No, no, no. We wait.' It was his turn to fold his arms.

But I could not hide my scorn. 'Wait, for what, old man? For our rescuers? I have no plans to spend the rest of my days down here—which would be about how long it would take for anyone to find us.' Now there was a thought I wish I had not articulated. I rambled on, my anger gathering steam. 'I have things to do and places to be. You may not mind waiting for a rescue party that will never come, but I plan to get out of here alive.' Well, that wasn't much better, but surely he would have to agree.

He paid me no mind, but kept feeding wood into the fire. 'You want to climb out? Go ahead. I will wait.'

I wanted to strangle him, but why bother. I would send a search crew if he still would not come when I got to the top. Shaking my head wearily, I turned, slung my backpack over my shoulders and looked up toward the vague source of light which indicated the mouth of the cave. I quelled an unpleasant tingle in my belly and looked for a hand-hold in the right direction. I grasped a likely looking root and hoisted myself up the slope. My boot scraped the wall a bit until it found purchase, and I stretched my arm up for the next grip. The fire crackled behind me and I tried not to think that it sounded like cackling, although I could not stop myself from picturing the old man grinning at my back. I had just raised myself another meter higher when the walls of the cavern began to groan and shiver. I clamped harder onto the roots in my hands, but I had no confidence that I would be able to hold for long—not if this kept up. Perhaps it would pass. I clung tightly, counting under my breath. But there was no doubt: the rumbles were getting louder and the shakes stronger. I gasped when my left hand lost its grip and I could have sworn that I heard the old man chuckle, but it would have been impossible to hear it (I must be charitable) in that cacophony. I did at least real-ize—if not hear—my own strangled yelp of frustration as I fell back to the slick floor of the cavern and rolled neatly to the old man's feet.

He did not crow 'I told you so,' but offered his hand to help me climb to my feet. I tried in vain to brush off the muck from the walls. It caked on my elbows and knees and covered me with its putrid stench.

'I told you to wait,' old Väinö said, shaking his head at my youthful impetuousness. I was too angry to speak. But as the shaking continued, I decided to hold my breath. He would not hear my withering retort over the resounding tremors anyway.

All at once the whole cavern seemed to pitch. Reaching out for a handhold, I grabbed the old man's arm and together we turned asses-up. He seemed to think it a jolly trick, but I was totally disgusted. The putrefaction from the walls covered us and the stink filled my nose—and ears and eyes, I could have sworn. It was everywhere.

The rumbling grew louder now, and the whole cave shook. Who would believe an earthquake here! If we are even still in the same country—perhaps I have fallen all the way to Russia. The horrible noise! I thought earthquakes were just shaking, but this terrible noise—almost like speech, if a cavern could bellow.

Of course the old trickster decided to jump on that thought train. 'It's Vipunen's anger—he can't bear this fire in his belly,' he said gleefully. Oh my god, it all came back to me at last from my childhood memories. Vipunen was a giant. This old man really thinks he is *vaka vanha* Väinämöinen! Of course, and how clever he has been to wake the sleeping giant. The fact that his 'giant' is an unstable mountain crater doesn't bother him! If I were not so busy trying to keep my feet, I would certainly give him a piece of my mind—and not the kindly piece of it either.

He shook his fist at the walls then gave them a random kick. 'That's right! Your belly's burning and there's nothing you can do about it!' He cackled wildly, heedless of the filth covering his tunic and the smell that filled up our nostrils. He grinned at me. 'He is cursing me and all the creatures who walk the land. He will curse from now until midnight. But we will stoke the fire. We will give him no respite!'

True to his word he turned and fed the fire faster, thrusting wood into the flames with a manic glee. All the while the walls trembled and the cave rumbled louder. No doubt it would soon fall around our ears—an alarming thought. Would Anikka cry to hear that I had died so? Or would she dry her eyes oh so quickly on Matti's strong shoulders, with his ponytail and his smooth words of comfort? Suddenly I felt compelled to rise once more and take charge of the situation.

'Old man!' I shouted, forgetting my politeness in my rage. 'We've got to get out of here before we die!'

'Oh, we won't die,' he said more calmly. 'But I'm not going anywhere until I learn at least a hundred charms from Vipunen. You hear that, old man!' His gaze lowered, his eyes agleam once more with mischief. 'In fact, I think I quite like it here. Your liver is going to make a fine repast. Your belly fat will make the best smoked bacon—and such a roast I will make from your thick knotted lungs.' He turned and his eye lighted on some branches lying a little further away. 'More fire, more—there's a feast to be made.' He cackled maniacally and threw the wood on the fire, continuing to look about for further fuel. The cave trembled more wildly and I grabbed hold of the brush growing from the walls to try to keep my feet.

From a withered pack the steadfast old one took a hammer and began to beat it upon one of the stumps, crying 'Here will be my forge! Here I'll strike my anvil until you bellow forth those charms that I have come for, the wily words of wisdom, the magic sayings only you know, the knowledge you have kept to yourself, hidden deep in these crevasses. Such understanding should not be kept a thousand leagues beneath the earth! Sing them to me!'

A thousand leagues? A thousand leagues! I began to feel faint. Something of the old man's madness was starting to take hold of my tired brain. A thousand leagues, indeed, but I could not work up a sufficient amount of rage. Damn his wild words, the mad pounding! It was beginning to take its toll. I would do anything, anything to get him to stop that horrid noise, the terrible trembling of the cavern walls. I was only grateful there was nothing in my stomach to vomit forth, or it would have been sprayed across the walls of this hellhole. Only I must beg him, stop stop stop that infernal cacophony. With a valiant effort, I struggled to my feet if only to fall across his wiry body and halt that tireless hammering arm.

Then the cave gave a spasm and suddenly was still. I held my breath and all at once the abrupt silence—which seemed at once deafening—gave way to a new sound. Väinö dropped his hammer and craned his neck to listen, too.

It must have been the wind.

What else could it be? It whistled down the cavern's throat to meet us and carried a weave of sounds. Surely it was the madness, the time alone in the cave with the crazed old man, the ancient rune singer, but I could almost swear I heard—

Singing?

It was really almost like a voice, a voice that cried through the bristly innards of the grotto, picking up the scratchings of a thousand branches, swiping the sweat from the dripping walls until it reached us and sounded, damned if it didn't, like words, like speech.

A rough voice, true; one that sighed a thousand years unheard, only to croak and wheeze now, slowly gathering strength. The echoes built around us, resonating louder now. In that blustering windy noise I heard the words of a thousand charms, as if arising from ancient depths: heard the cry from the very birth of time itself, heard the word that spoke beginning, said 'air' and it was so, voiced 'water' and it sprang forth, all the earth giving life; Ilmatar descending from the air, to shape the world, to birth the singer; every charm and every spell from the sun to the moon, from the earth to the sky, from Ukko to Rauni; from the belly of Vipunen to Väinämöinen's ear, all enchantments flowed.

I must have been mad.

But old Väinö smiled so broadly I thought the top of his head might just fall off. He knocked the fiery pyre into the waters and quenched its licking orange tongues. Rubbing his hands together joyfully, he turned once more to me. I know I must have looked a sight, rattled by the echoing winds and rocked by who-knows-what strange earthquakes. It was the darkness, the lack of food, the disorienting feeling of being underground that left me gasping for breath and, let's face it, delirious. Voices, indeed! And yet—the memory made me shiver then, even as it does now. For a moment it

was possible to believe that we were indeed in the body of
the giant Vipunen, gathering charms for the venerable rune
singer.

Bah! Simple hunger can cause delusions of a surprising
nature, or so the ranger who found me later explained. I was
caught up in the old man's delusions, my brain was weak-
ened with low blood sugar and my pulse was racing without
sufficient nutrients. And the old codger did not make things
any easier, pretending to be talking to that deep-mouthed
cave.

'Open up your jaws much wider, Antero Vipunen, if you
wish to get this frisking food out of your belly today. Come
now, don't make us wait, or we'll have to start another fire
to cook our dinner!' He had the audacity to wink at me, as
if I shared his mad fantasy. His shouting caused the cavern
to tremble once more. Such madness—were we to be hurled
into a deeper shaft? It was truly more than I could bear.
Good-bye Anikka, I hope Matti is good to you—

Suddenly everything was tumult. Rocks crashed down
and winds whistled and bushes flattened and the whole
mountain groaned. This was it, I thought, we are going to
die! But all at once silence erupted and like a mother's smile
after a bad dream, a glimmer of sunshine misted down the
giant's gullet, amidst the rubble and the dust, and hope rose
in my breast.

'Come on, old man, now's our chance—before another
cave-in!' I grabbed old Väinö's hand and jerked him along
the rocky path upward. We scrabbled a hold on anything
in our sight, and even if the cliff-dwelling shrubs too often
revealed their shallow roots, there was always another just
beyond it to hold our grip, to give us just enough leverage
to claw our way toward the light. Closer and closer—how
could we have not escaped before this, I thought uselessly.
Why, the way to the surface could not have been much
more than a hundred meters! Funny we could not see the
light before. Unless the tremors had opened it wider; yes,
surely that must be the answer. Nearly there; the old man
puffing behind me—those ridiculous birch bark shoes!
Thank goodness for my Ibex, they gripped the ground like
sure-foot goats. I saw sky! We were free!

We had such momentum we both rolled out of the

mouth of the cave, lithe as a pair of golden martens, and collapsed, laughing with relief. Sun! Sky! Freedom! I did my best to slap the dust and slime out of my clothes, and the old one did the same. If my face was a grimy as his though, there was little to be done to salvage any dignity, so I laughed good and loud, even though I knew I would never get all this goo out of my beautiful Ibex. Ever companionable, steadfast old Väinö joined in the hilarity, though he could hardly know it was his own besmirched face that doubled my laughter. I got out my flask of water—no more need for rationing—and drank deeply, wiped my mouth and offered it to my august companion, who likewise celebrated our hard-won freedom by relishing a long draught.

The ancient rune singer handed back my flask, a thoughtful look taking over his face. 'Oh, no fear now, old man,' I said. 'We have escaped certain death in that unstable chamber. This is a time to celebrate.' Heavens, don't let him have a heart attack now! These old ones can be rather fragile.

He knitted his brow and patted the belt around his generous waist. 'I think I left my hammer down there,' he said musingly. Did he actually—no!—want to go back into that hellhole?! With that foul smell and that sharp descent—I felt my brow grow warm at the thought of returning to the cave, the belly of Vipunen. It must have been the lack of food that made my scalp feel so light and made the sky swim overhead, the low blood sugar—

And that is how I got a second bump on my head.

Laura Stark has written extensively about Finnish folk tradi-tions, notably about the traditions of women. I've been fascinated by her studies, and I thought it would be great to see how those traditions might continue on and get passed around today beyond Finnish families.

Raising Lempi

'Oh, my god, this feels sooo good!' Karin groaned.

Leena smiled. 'I told you it would. And you were so reluctant!'

'You're never going to get me out of here, I can tell you now,' Deirdre added. 'I'm just going to have all my mail sent right here.' She let out a sigh of utter contentment. The fresh wood of the sauna walls still gave off a hint of forest wildness. Or maybe it was the birch twigs Leena had gathered for them which perfumed the warm sanctuary. The sauna had the double illusion of enclosed safety and wild scents. If the women closed their eyes, they could easily imagine themselves in the middle of a forest.

'I think my husband needs to build one of these, too,' Maria added. 'I think it would be a wonderful way to escape from the children—and a good way to fire the passions!'

The other three laughed, although Deirdre insisted, 'I feel so languid. Sex is the last thing on my mind at the moment.'

Leena stretched her arms above her head. The sweat was already trickling down her back and between her breasts. 'The best thing, of course, is to run out naked into the snow and dive through the ice into the lake. Then you feel like a little loving!'

'Frozen lake?' Maria shook her head. 'I don't think so! I still can't take the cold up here. Down in Honduras we got the heat, but never this kind of cold.' She shivered despite the warm caress of the sauna. 'Well, maybe up in the mountains, but I'm a coastal gal.'

'Finnish tradition!' Leena said. 'The hottest sauna you can stand, then the coldest water. Of course, afterward you need a big glass of vodka! There's an old saying, '*Jos vessi, vodka ja sauna ei auta, on tauti kolemaksi*'—which means,' she amended, chuckling at their quizzical looks, "If water, vodka and sauna don't help, the condition is mortal." More laughter rang around the small room as the last of the long day's stress vanished.

'So, the sauna must be the throbbing sexual center of life in Finland,' Karin said, trying not to think about how many months it had been since her last memorable date. 'No wonder you're supposed to be naked!'

Leena shook her head. 'My grandmother always said you were to behave in the sauna as you did in church. No loud voices, no running around, no horseplay. The sauna was a sacred place.'

'*Sow-na.* I didn't even realize it was pronounced like that,' Karin said.

'You know, that sounds kind of like the Garifuna people's tradition,' Maria said. 'They have a kind of spiritual bath for the souls of the kindly ancestors. One of my best friends back home is Garifuna—she took me to some celebrations once and explained everything. It was really beautiful—the songs especially.'

'But don't they also deliver babies in the sauna?' Deirdre asked. 'I'm sure I read that somewhere, maybe in the *National Geographic*. Wow, if you'd had this when I was still pumping out the tykes, I'd have never left!'

'Eww,' Karin said, shifting a little on her towel. 'That's gross!'

Leena smiled. 'Actually it was the cleanest and most hygienic place to give birth. For centuries the sauna was used for birthing children, for smoking food, for healing just about anything. There are herbs you can add to the water so the *löyly*—that's the steam—has even more beneficial properties. But the *löyly* itself is thought to have great healing properties.'

'Centuries?' Deirdre let out a sigh and leaned back further. 'I thought people didn't bathe back then.'

'They did in Finland!' Leena said. 'All around the Baltic, in fact, even though in later years the reformers tried to get them to stop.'

'Why would they want them to stop bathing?' Karin asked. 'I'd think they would equate a clean body with a clean mind—I know my mother always did.'

Leena chuckled in agreement. 'I guess it was because they thought there was something inherently pagan in the sauna traditions—and, well, I suppose anything with naked flesh was suspect to some degree.'

'And where women were alone, doing mysterious things like giving birth,' Maria added. 'I'm sure they wanted to make sure the women were not up to their old superstitious ways.'

Leena nodded. 'Oh, undoubtedly! There were so many old traditions associated with the sauna, practices the church probably wanted to discourage as myths—'

'Or maybe they were afraid they weren't myths!' Deirdre cut in. 'No room for more than one god. The old ones had to go.'

Karin lifted one of the birch whisks and shook it. 'Let me guess, these had something to do with magic, right?'

Everyone laughed, but Leena explained. 'Actually, the *vihta* help get the circulation going. More sweat opens the pores, leaves you cleaner.'

Karin playfully whacked Maria, who swiftly retaliated with the whisk by her side, until Deirdre said with mock severity, 'Like church, girls! Remember, you're supposed to behave like you do in church.'

'This is how I behaved in church,' Maria laughed. 'That's why Mamá was always yelling at us. '*Cállate! Siéntate!* You'll make the Virgin cry!"

'But it can't just be health,' Deirdre insisted. 'There's got to be a history of magic, too. Hidden rituals of women. Where women gather together out of the sight of men, there's always some sharing of secret knowledge.' She winked at her friends, thinking of the many secrets they had all shared over the years.

'Health was always the main concern. You know, you're all losing about three or four hundred calories just sitting here,' Leena said. They all cheered enthusiastically. 'But you're right, of course. There were some traditional magical rites that happened in the sauna, too.'

'Sex magic!' Deirdre was triumphant.

'Well—'

'C'mon, Leena. Spill!'

'There is this one thing my grandmother told me about, a tradition. It's called 'Raising Lempi."

'Wasn't he one of the Three Stooges?' Deirdre cracked.

'Very funny. What's it about?' Maria asked curiously.

Leena stretched again, closing her eyes and casting her mind back to her grandmother's words. 'It was for girls whose *lempi* seemed to need a boost.'

'What's 'lempi'? Explain!'

'Well, it's kind of hard to define exactly—it's like attractiveness, I guess, but usually with the aim of getting a husband.'

'So, like a kind of love magic?' Maria suggested.

'Well, no—not exactly. There were love potions too—usually putting a little of yourself into a cake or coffee.'

'Oh, don't tell me—' Karin started.

'Um...well, yeah, it was usually some of your menstrual blood.'

'Gross!'

'But supposedly it worked like a charm—so to speak,' Leena continued. 'The man who ate the cake or drank the special coffee would not be able to think of anything else until he had married you and had you in his farmstead.'

Deirdre laughed. 'Then he woke up and said, 'What the hell happened to me!''

Leena nodded. 'But raising lempi was different, not so coercive. It was just increasing your attractiveness so you got more suitors, then you could have your choice.'

Karin raised her hand. 'Me, me! I need that! I think my lempi has fallen down about to my ankles. How *do* we raise my lempi?' She tried to ignore the chorus of giggling. 'I'm serious—at this point I'm willing to try anything.'

Leena considered for a moment. 'Well, I don't recall the details too clearly. I know it had something to do with the *väki* of the fire, its power, somehow getting transferred to the girl. To power her lempi, I guess.'

'And we do get to beat her with the whisks, right?' Deirdre asked.

'Why not! Hmmm. There were rhymes they repeated, about pairs and things that go together—'

'Like salt and pepper?'

Leena shook her head. 'No, usually more suggestive things. It was in private, right? So they were much more blunt.' Deirdre giggled with sudden amusement at the thought.

'All right,' said Karin, standing up. 'Let's do it!' The others each grabbed her *vihta* and stood before her.

'Um—how shall we start?' They looked to Leena. She grinned and felt a bit foolish, but plunged right in. 'Okay, um, let's see. We call on the power of the fire's *väki* to reinvigorate—'

'Ooh, good word!' Deirdre said.

'Shhh!' Karin scolded. 'Don't interrupt!'

Leena laughed. 'We call on the power of the fire's *väki* to reinvigorate Karin's lempi.' She whisked her friend and the others joined in, laughing with delight. 'May her lempi rise to new heights and draw to her new lovers. Like moths to a flame—'

'Like a hand in a glove!' Maria said.

'Like a rabbit in its burrow,' Deirdre chimed in.

'Like a key in a lock!'

'Like a foot in a sock!'

'More lempi, higher, higher!' Karin said excitedly.

The others took up the chant, 'More lempi, more lempi, higher, higher,' circling Karin and slapping her with the birch twigs. When their joyous laughter seemed to have reached its peak, Leena splashed another ladle of water over the rocks, producing another burst of *löyly*, which was accompanied by the whoops of the other women who collapsed after that small exertion in the sweltering chamber.

'Do you think it worked?' Karin asked, breathlessly.

Leena took in her friend's sparkling eyes and flushed cheeks and smiled. Deirdre slapped Karin's thighs once more—'For good luck!'—and sat back down, sighing. 'That's some ritual, Leena.'

'Well, I don't know if that's exactly how it was supposed to go—Grandma wasn't giving instruction, after all.' She laughed, adding, 'but look at you, Karin. You're positively glowing!'

'That's just sweat,' Karin said, but her smile broadened.

'No,' Maria corrected. 'Horses sweat, men perspire, women glow. You are definitely glowing, girl.'

'I'll bet you've already got a couple calls on your cell by now, asking you out for drinks tonight,' Deirdre said.

'Let's go check,' Leena said. 'It's about time we cooled off.

I have some nice cold chardonnay in the ice bucket on the patio.'

'No vodka?' Karin asked as they gathered up their towels.

'I've got it if you want it, but wait until you see how light-headed you get from just a little wine after this.'

'Yeah, that lempi—it goes straight to your head, huh?'

Leena laughed, but nodded as she turned down the dial on the thermostat. 'The sauna is like that. Leaves you a bit off kilter the first time.'

'The sauna? Or the magic?' Karin grinned.

Leena looped her arm over her friend's shoulder. 'What makes you think there's a difference?'

The magical instrument of the Kalevala*! It is not possible to pick one up without being instantly charmed. Discovering the kantele led me back to playing and performing music, something I cannot believe I ever let go. I wanted to write a story that spoke to that mystique and to the power of the eternal sage Väinämöinen, who invented the kantele (both the pike bone and wooden versions) but who has notoriously bad luck with women.*

The Kantele

'Oh goodness, look!'

Kirsti drew her attention away from the age-browned hat box before her to see what her sister held up. 'What's that?'

Elina grinned with happy surprise. 'It's a kantele! Oh, wouldn't it be perfect for little Anni.' She was in raptures, but that was predictable enough. Everything at the *tori* had been met with the same enthusiasm. Ooh, the *pulla*! So warm and soft and raisiny, fresh from the oven. Ooh, the little wooden sauna signs! Never mind they didn't have a sauna. Ooh, the blue and white quilts, proudly brandishing Finnish pride. Now her sister had some new fancy—how much was it going to cost? The little market was becoming expensive; somehow Elina never managed to spend her own money.

Kirsti gave in to the inevitable tide of enthusiasm that oozed from her sister like melted butter, and she let herself be pulled to the next table, where a smiling older woman sat regally surveying her wares. 'What have you got there, Elina?'

It was the elderly woman who answered. Her name tag bore the title 'Marja' and she leaned forward with a smile. 'A very fine old kantele! Made from birch by my grandfather himself in Karelia. A finer instrument could not be whittled by Väinämöinen himself!'

Elina chimed in. 'Isn't it just darling? It's just the right size for Anni's little hands. Oh, look at the craftsmanship!'

The way she always went on about 'craftsmanship' generally gave people the impression that she was quite knowledgeable herself, although Kirsti could not remember a single craft project her sister had picked up that had not been dropped, unfinished, within a short while. But as she took the little kantele in her hands, Kirsti had to admit it was really lovely. The golden birch was finely worked with loving patience, and when she tentatively plucked a string it rang out like a bell, which surprised her. She had expected something more harp-like in its tone.

'It's the simplest thing to play for any child or adult, even one who feels she knows no music. Each of the five strings is in harmony with the others. You cannot play a wrong tune.' The woman was being quite persuasive. It was rather late in the day, Kirsti thought, then felt a tad uncharitable. No reason to assume the woman just wanted to unload this item. Here was this woman selling off her family treasures. Perhaps she had no one left with whom to share them.

'It's very charming. But surely you have some grandchildren who would love such an instrument?'

Marja shook her head and held out her hands helplessly. 'They care only for videogames. If I could plug it into a computer, well, maybe then they would be interested.' The three women laughed.

The longer Kirsti looked at the little harp, the more she felt inclined to take it. The curl of its tip swirled like icing, and the vaguely triangular shape was pleasing. It had been made with care, with delicately carved details here and there to delight the eye, even featuring a snowflake surrounding the sound hole. She braced herself before asking the price, but Marja offered a very reasonable one. Amidst Elina's delighted cries, she paid the friendly old woman, who thanked her heartily.

'It is enough to know it goes to a welcoming home,' Marja said with a note of regret in her voice. 'Your daughter will find that the instrument itself will teach her how to play. She need only spend time playing to become proficient.'

Kirsti smiled, but then frowned. 'How will we know how to tune it?'

Marja laughed and took a small scrap of paper. 'Here, I write down the notes, very easy: D, E, F#, G, A. You can tune it with any piano. Oh, and not to forget—' She reached into her apron pocket and fished out a small key that looked like it might fit a windup toy. 'This you use on the tuning pegs to get to the right tuning. Here.' She promptly demonstrated, loosening then tightening one string to return it to perfect pitch. Then she handed the instrument to Kirsti. 'May it bring much magic to your little daughter!'

'Aren't you glad I made you come along to the *tori*!' Elina was triumphantly certain that all thanks were due to her. Kirsti listened to her bubbly conversation all the way home with a practiced ear, allowing most of it to slide off like snow on a sunny March afternoon. But something her sister said caught her attention as they bumped along the country lanes.

'Wait. What was that you said about the pikebone?'

'I swear you never listen to a word I say,' Elina pouted but, finding her sister unwilling to bend, continued with her explanation. 'The first kantele, the first one he made—'

'Who made?'

Elina sighed. 'Väinämöinen, of course!'

'He's the old singer from myth, right?'

'Well, he's a lot more than that! But he made the first kantele from the jaw of a pike.'

Kirsti snorted. 'A fish's jaw? Must have been a tiny instrument.'

'It was a giant pike, you know, as things always are in this kind of origin story. But somehow the kantele got lost—in a battle, I think—so he made a new one from wood; and when he played, all the animals and all the people gathered round to hear him play. It was magic.'

'It does have a lovely sound,' Kirsti said diplomatically. She could tell that Elina was going to go off on one of her excited travelogues of myth and mystery, which made her glad they were almost to her apartment. Kirsti waved and drove off while her sister continued to chatter on the sidewalk, only half listening to herself. Kirsti drove the remaining blocks home with a vague smile on her face, anticipating a pleasant reception from her daughter. Mike would be happy enough with the sweet bread, which had filled the car with the pleasant aroma of cardamom.

'I smell *pulla*!' Mike called from the kitchen.

'So do I,' yelled Anni, who was drawing her latest masterpiece with crayons.

'Put a pot of coffee on and we'll have some, but let's not spoil dinner,' Kirsti said as she dropped the bag on the table and gave her husband a quick kiss. 'What is for dinner, anyway?'

'Lizard head!' Anni offered.

'The little toe of a frog,' Mike added.

Kirsti smiled. 'Lucky me. I hope we have plenty of choc-olate sauce to cover up the flavor.' She reached into the other bag and looked at her daughter. 'Guess what I have?'

Anni grinned and dropped the purple crayon with which she had been coloring a horse. 'A present? For me!'

'If you know the magic word.'

'Please!'

Kirsti pulled out the kantele and handed it to her daugh-ter, who looked at it, puzzled, but remembered to murmur, 'Thank you, Mommie.'

'It's called a 'kantele,' Anni. A kind of lap harp from Finland. You play it by plucking the strings.' Kirsti demon-strated with a clumsy scale.

Anni clapped her hands together, then tried it herself, laughing with delight at the sound it made. She immediately began to try the strings in different orders, making her own little melodies. Kirsti and Mike exchanged a smile. 'The very first one was made from a giant pike's bone,' Kirsti said to the dutifully bent head of her daughter, 'by Väinämöinen, the great sage of the *Kalevala* stories.'

'Sage is a spice,' Anni said without taking her eyes off the strings.

'A different kind of sage,' Mike said laughing. 'As a rule. What amazing craftsmanship,' he enthused, running a finger along the soundboard.

Kirsti smiled. From her husband the carpenter that was a compliment indeed. Never mind 'measure twice, cut once'; he measured at least three times and in different weather conditions to account for swelling. 'You know, Elina said the same thing.'

'For once, we agree.'

Anni did not tire of the kantele after dinner, returning to its lively tunes as soon as she had washed her hands. Instead of a bedtime story, she generously offered to play a tune of her own composition for her parents, which she proudly accom-plished after several false starts and muttered expressions of 'Wait, wait, I've got it now.' Kirsti drew the line at actually allowing her daughter to sleep with the instrument in her bed, so Anni had to content herself with seeing it sitting on the bureau as she fell asleep, a warm smile still on her lips.

'So, do we have the next Sibelius?' Mike whispered as they pattered down the stairs.

'I can't believe how she took to it. I guess that woman Marja was right, it really is simple enough to play. Even so, I've never seen her so dedicated, not even to her drawings.' Evidence of the latter devotion festooned the refrigerator and every spare space on the wall of Mike's workroom. They had been sure there was a budding Rembrandt in training, if not a Vernon Ward. Anni was awfully fond of ducks for some reason and had drawn flocks of the creatures over the last several weeks. She and Mike had kidded each other that the eyes did indeed follow you around the room, which was a bit unsettling while he was planing or sanding in the workshop.

'It really worked like magic, that kantele,' Mike said.

Kirsti wondered at the repetition of that word. Such an odd word to encounter so many times in one day. Must be the effect of the kantele, she thought. Maybe there was a little bit of the enchantment from the old myths alive in its strings after all.

The next morning she was not as surprised to find Anni carrying the small harp to the breakfast table, although she managed to convince her to stop playing long enough to have some pulla with her juice. Once her dishes were put away in the dishwasher and her hands scrupulously washed—her father told her dirty hands would make the strings rust and break—Anni took the kantele in hand and ran outside to plant herself under the apple tree to play.

'Maybe we have the next Mozart,' Mike said, wrapping his arms around Kirsti's shoulders and kissing her cheek. 'I'm off to the workshop to be this year's cabinetry sensation. What's the schedule for you?'

Kirsti sighed. 'I think it's laundry time.'

When the load of towels was ready to dry the sun was brightly shining, Kirsti took the basket outside to hang on the line. The pleasant days had lasted much further into September than anyone had predicted—weather profession-

als included—and it seemed a shame not to take advantage
of this last leisurely Indian summer. Besides, she would be
able to hear Anni's playing, which was sure to be lovely.

Kirsti was puzzled at first to not see her daughter anywhere in the yard, but then she heard low voices by the
garden. Must be Patti or Selma from next door, she sur-
mised; but when she came around the hedges there was only
Anni. She was sitting on the arbor bench, her head turned
as if she were speaking to someone next to her. 'Anni?' Kirsti
called out.

'Hello, Mommie! Look what I learned to play.' Anni
bent her head down and with studied concentration slowly
plucked out a little tune that was instantly familiar. Kirsti
knew it was on the CD of *Kalevala* runos Elina had cajoled
her into buying at another *tori*, but she couldn't recall which
song it was. Her moment of confusion evaporated with
sudden pride. Anni could play a tune by ear! It was certainly
more than she could do herself. Elina sang like a lark, but
Kirsti couldn't carry a tune with monogrammed luggage, as
her father always said. Anni looked up with an infectious
grin as Kirsti walked over to sit beside her. 'Did you like it,
Mommie?'

'It was wonderful. Can you play it again?'

'Yes, of course. Listen!' And at once she set to playing
again, and Kirsti marveled at the quick study. It really was
quite like—there, the word wanted to rise up once more:
magic. Kirsti frowned and thought about having heard
two voices when she came out with the laundry. She must
have been mistaken, that's all there was to it. The tinkling
tones of the strings soon soothed her spirit once more and
she grinned delightedly as her daughter played in the late
summer sun. It made the chore of laundry pass much more
quickly.

'Have you seen what a genius my daughter is?' Kirsti said
to Mike when he issued forth from his workshop, sawdust
in his hair.

'What's for lunch?' Mike asked, going to the fridge for
some lemonade. 'Is there any of that smoked ham left?'

'Aren't you going to ask why my daughter's such a
genius?' Kirsti said to his backside as he rummaged in the
meat drawer.

He emerged once more, ham-handed. 'I already know my daughter's a genius. Why wouldn't she be?'

'Do you know she's already learned a tune or two by heart—playing them by ear, that is.'

Mike chortled. 'She *is* a genius, what with two tone deaf parents. Must have skipped a generation. Where's the good mustard?'

Kirsti reached into the door of the fridge before it swung closed and grabbed the jar. 'Here. Now aren't you pleased?'

'Yes, dear,' he said with a quick kiss. 'Thank you for the mustard.'

'No, I mean about Anni being able to play so quickly.'

Mike slathered a good bit of the mustard on a slab of pumpernickel. 'Didn't the old woman say it was very easy to play? Maybe we shouldn't get our hopes up for a second Mozart. After all, the harp's only got five notes.'

Kirsti closed the mustard jar, her hands moving absently, automatically. 'It's not that. It's just…' She felt silly mentioning the strange sensation of hearing a second voice conversing with Anni outside. It was probably just acoustics. Sounds often echoed around in strange ways, right? Mike was looking at her expectantly, waiting for her to finish her sentence. 'I'm just pleased. That she can pick things up by ear.'

'Me too, hon.' Mike bestowed another kiss and took his sandwich back to his woodworking. Kirsti stood in the kitchen for a few minutes, arms crossed. The CD, she finally thought. Where was it? She headed to the front room, where a jumble of CDs filled one shelf. After pawing through a bunch of 80s hair bands and bemoaning Mike's bad taste in music for the umpteenth time, she found it.

Kantele Treasures: that CD from the *tori*. Elina had admired it greatly and as usual was more than willing to get Kirsti to spend money on something. Though she hadn't listened to it in some months, Kirsti enjoyed it whenever she happened upon it in the pile of CDs. The soothing tones of the instruments were always a welcome balm. She had forgotten that the little five string was the same kind of harp as the big concert kanteles featured on most of the tracks of the album and pictured on the back of the package. She flipped it over and found a fanciful-looking painting of an old man in a skullcap playing a kantele, sitting on a boulder and surrounded by maidens of some kind. She looked at the liner notes. Of course, it was old Väinämöinen himself in the painting. Kirsti examined the bearded figure closely. 'I guess you can get a bevy of maidens at any age if you know magic,' she muttered to no one in particular.

The first song was the one she had heard Anni play; she was certain of it even before she put the disc into the player. 'Vaka vanha Väinämöinen,' sure enough. Kirsti recognized the simple tune about the eternal sage even as it grew into variations and harmonies with more complicated harps and arrangements. Anni must have heard the song, too, and remembered it. Remarkable what children pick up from the environment.

She almost told Mike that night about her worries over the oddness of Anni's preternatural skill, but the thoughts sounded silly even to her own ears. The chances of their daughter possessing some kind of mysterious ability, after all, was pretty slim—and those of hearing impossible conversations was downright anorexic. Why not just be enchanted with her daughter's skill and leave it at that?

The next day, however, her concerns returned. Kirsti was walking down the hall and thought she heard a few notes on the kantele. The problem was that Anni was in day school. Kirsti poked her head in Anni's room and saw the kantele where her daughter had left it, on the center of her neatly made bed. She walked over and plucked its strings a bit, recalling myriad detective stories where the inspector would pronounce a gun still warm to the touch and know the suspect was nearby. The strings, though, were cool to the touch. In addition to the carving on the soundboard, she noticed, the snowflake motif continued around the sides of the instrument. The warm honey tone of the pine was clearly marked by age, although the strings were a shiny new silver. Kirsti plucked the middle string and the tone lingered in the air, seemingly endlessly. Eventually she laid the kantele back on the bed. 'You're being very silly,' she told herself.

When Anni got home she went straight to the kantele and began to play. Kirsti recognized the strains of 'Vaka vanha Väinämöinen' immediately, but soon she realized that her daughter had begun to pick out another tune, somewhat haltingly. 'What's that song, honey?' Kirsti said, poking her head around the door to her daughter's room. Out of the corner of her eye, she could have sworn she saw a figure melt away from sight, but there was nothing there but a few plush animals and Anni's book bag. Even if someone had been there, where could they have gone? Into Anni's closet? There was no one there now but her daughter, head bent over the instrument with serious concentration as she hesitatingly plucked a series of notes. 'What's the song, honey?' Kirsti repeated.

Anni looked up. 'I don't know its name, but I hear it in my head.' She returned her gaze back to the strings and patiently repeated the sequence. It wasn't quite right, but it was close. Nonetheless, her fingers slowed and finally stopped. 'I can't hear it now, Mommie,' Anni said after a few minutes of trying.

'Play the other one, sweetie. I know the name of that one. It's called 'Vaka vanha Väinämöinen.' We have it on a CD. Do you remember that one?' Kirsti became aware that she was staring at her daughter a little too intently, but the girl didn't seem to notice. She was still concentrating on the kantele, and slowly the notes to the familiar runo tune came forth once again. After Anni played the simple song through a couple of times, she suddenly began to sing.

In Finnish, Kirsti realized with sudden anxiety. Finnish! She herself knew at most a few dozen words, most of them the usual bunch of polite phrases learned from older relatives: *kiitos paljon*, *hyvää ilta*, or *kippis*. Yet Anni sang along confidently even as she twanged the strings with growing facility. A part of Kirsti's mind said it was the CD, that's all. She must have remembered the words from hearing it and retained them subconsciously. It was a calming thought that allowed her to dismiss the preternatural ability her daughter was exhibiting with this instrument.

Until she remembered that the whole disc had been instrumentals.

That was what made Kirsti try to talk to Mike about the incident later. He was usually understanding about her vague discontents, but that night he was distracted. Maybe,

Kirsti just had to admit, maybe it was because her story was simply ludicrous. 'But doesn't it seem impossible?' she asked finally, willing him to be as worried as she had been.

'Kids retain things in totally illogical ways,' Mike insisted, yawning noisily and snuggling down decisively. 'She probably just remembers it from the old church ladies. You could be paying beaucoup bucks for language training and not getting results that good. She's just got a knack for it, like I do for woodwork. Relax, honey.'

But the fears would not be quelled. The next day Anni was out in the garden again, playing away. This time Kirsti was more watchful. When she heard what seemed to be voices from the hedges where Anni sat, Kirsti stole up as quietly as she could and peeked through the branches.

There he was, leaning over Anni, humming along with her playing. Kirsti finally understood what people meant by seeing red, because her vision filled with a furious crimson. What was that odd old man doing with her daughter?! With an effort, she restrained herself from immediately rushing toward them—would he fade into the bushes?—stopping to study the interloper carefully. Although he matched the picture on the CD in general strokes, the real Väinämöinen – she felt, instinctively, that it *must* be him – looked both much older and much more intimidating. While the romantic painting made him look like a jolly grandfather, this man exuded an air of roguish knowing, almost contempt that gave her an unpleasant jolt. From the top of his skull cap to his curly birch shoes, he was a walking anachronism. But he was real. She could hear him, she could see him—and so could Anni.

'Who's your friend?' she asked Anni, stepping forward. Kirsti tried to make her voice sound as natural as possible, burying her panic through sheer force of will. The old man glanced up at her, cool as a trout stream.

'Hello, Kirsti,' he said, as if they had been friends since the world began. 'Your daughter is very talented. A natural, you might say.' There was a twinkle in his eye that meant to reassure, but Kirsti was not at all pleased with the old man. She was beginning to suspect that he would not be easy to get rid of any time soon.

'Oh, don't be so modest. You certainly seemed to have helped along that natural talent,' Kirsti said, keeping her eye on her daughter who was still playing, head bent as she concentrated on the strings.

'It is my joy to mentor the young,' the wise old shaman said. 'A young girl needs so much guidance.'

'That's what she has parents for,' Kirsti said, flushing a little, unable to contain her irritation any longer. 'Those who love her know what's best.'

'Ah, but the wisdom of the ages is on my side,' the eternal sage countered. 'There is so much I can teach her.'

'I can make you go away.' The words felt hollow in her mouth, however, and the old man just smiled smugly.

'You cannot keep her away from me,' Väinämöinen said. There was a friendly tone to the words, a smile still resting on his lips, but Kirsti felt a chill.

Whatever was at work here she was powerless to stop. Say it, she told herself, feeling numb. Magic, it's magic—it's not happy fairies and godmothers magic, but it was magic all the same.

Anni was looking up now, her brow furrowed in puzzlement. Her eyes darted back and forth from her mother to her new friend. 'Play a little more, sweetie,' Kirsti said, unsure of what to do, but certain that panicking her daughter would serve no purpose. Anni dutifully leaned her head over the strings and began to strum away at a lively tune. Kirsti sighed and closed her eyes in frustration. When she opened them again he was gone.

* * *

That night Kirsti lay awake while Mike snorted next to her, murmuring about measuring shingles that didn't seem to fit. Her head seemed too full of things. What to do, what to do? She had to protect her child, that was clear—but what was she protecting her from? An old man in a funny hat with a strangely magical ability to appear and disappear at will, and to make her daughter something of a prodigy on this ancient instrument. The fact that he brought joy to Anni tempered her concerns a little, but not enough. Kirsti sat up, hugging her knees. This was not acceptable. She had

thought of telling Mike, but how could she explain something that she could hardly believe herself. What was there
to do? She had nothing.

No, that wasn't entirely true. Kirsti threw back the covers
and hopped out of bed. Where was it? She went over to the
bookshelf and scanned the titles. There! The thick book's
gilded cover was a little dusty, but she knew it immediately.
Her mother had given her this copy of *The Kalevala* when
she and Mike had married, fearful that Kirsti would somehow lose her heritage once she was joined to someone who
wasn't a Finn. She had barely cracked it open during their
ten years together.

Kirsti flipped to the table of contents. She looked for the
first chapter with his name in it, 'Väinämöinen's Promise.'
Scanning the lines of poetry she was surprised to find the
wise old sage crying, lost and far from home. This was the
man who frightened her? Why would he be weeping? She
turned the pages and then saw his speech about regretting
that he had ever left home, how a stranger could not heal
the heart like those at home. Ah, this was the story that led
to his promising the Sampo to Louhi, witch of the North,
because she said she could return him to his home. Oh,
and her daughter, too—oh wait, that was to Ilmarinen,
his friend, the smith who actually forged the Sampo. But
hadn't there been another young woman promised to
Väinämöinen?

Aino! That was it. Kirsti found the runo with her name
and read the words swiftly. Rather than marry the ancient
one, the maiden Aino threw herself into the waves. Her
blood flowed into the waters, her flesh became fish, her ribs
driftwood on the water's shore. And what did her suitor do?
Wise old Väinämöinen, the eternal sage? He wept. Again he
wept! Kirsti marveled. She remembered other stories, tales
of his great accomplishments, but these accounts of his fail-
ures filled her with a renewed hope, though she wasn't yet
quite sure why.

Kirsti certainly didn't want her daughter throwing herself
into a lake to get away from the old man. But he sure didn't
seem to have much luck with women, did he?. Kirsti felt a
smile tug at the corners of her mouth. She wasn't sure what
his disappointments added up to, but they seemed to tip a

balance in her favor. Putting the book back in its place on the shelf, Kirsti turned to crawl back into bed beside Mike, who mumbled something about veneer and returned to snoring.

In the morning, Kirsti kept quietly watchful. Anni ran around the living room playing with her horses, and all was serene. After a mid-morning snack, however, Anni wandered down to her room and picked up the kantele to play. Kirsti forced herself to pause and listen to the sweet music for a few minutes before sneaking down the corridor. At first, she heard nothing but the bell-like tones resounding through the quiet house. Then Anni's soft voice began to sing, quickly joined by the powerful baritone of her mysterious friend. Kirsti squelched an urge to lunge protectively forward. The two voices blended together well; how easy it would be to be bound by the magic of their harmony.

Taking a deep breath, Kirsti rounded the corner. Anni did not look up, but Väinämöinen did. His look was slightly roguish, as if he had been caught doing something naughty, though not actually sorry to be found out. The two sat together on the little bed, surrounded by dolls, bears and a baby seal. Anni's legs drummed the side of the bed gently in time as she played. Kirsti crossed to the purple ottoman that served as Anni's chair and sat herself down to listen. Golden hair framed her daughter's face, her mouth a small frown of concentration, eyes locked onto her busy fingers as they produced a more complicated piece. With a start, Kirsti realized that Väinämöinen had produced a kantele from somewhere and was now strumming softly in accompaniment. The two instruments sang together with the sweetness of the cuckoo's call.

When the song finished, Kirsti laughed and clapped for the two musicians. Anni grinned, and the old man looked up with something approaching a smile, his craggy face crinkling a little to make way for the expression. His eyes were a crisp robin's egg blue, bluer than the faded cap on his head. How ancient he was, Kirsti thought. No, more than that – he was outside time. Fear crept back into her heart, but Kirsti refused to let it take root. She couldn't do anything about him, but there was someone who could. After all, she had raised her daughter to be her own self, independent and strong—and with a mile wide streak of *sisu*, that stubborn courage for which Finns were renowned

'Let's play the cuckoo song,' Anni said, tapping the strings lightly.

'No, let us play the new moon song. Your mother will like that one.' Kirsti knew that one, the story of the new bride coming to the village of her new husband, full of anxious hope. Väinämöinen smiled over at Anni, but the girl did not smile back.

'Cuckoo song,' she repeated. 'I want to play the cuckoo song.' Kirsti thrilled at her daughter's confident contention. Anni struck the first notes and continued on. Eventually, the old man bent his head and followed the tune with his fingers. Kirsti watched his face. He hid any annoyance he might have felt, but his expression was so carefully neutral that she thought he had to be irked. It brought a swift smile to her lips, which she tried just as quickly to disguise. Elementals, immortals—they had one disadvantage: they didn't change and grow like human beings. Väinämöinen would always be the same, always the eternal sage.

And he would always be unlucky with women.

"Kylä vuotti uutta kuuta' now?' the old man asked, taking up a querulous tone. He wanted his request played. He wanted control.

Anni nodded and smiled at her mother. 'You like that one, Mommie?'

Kirsti nodded. 'I just love to hear you play, my sweet.'

Väinämöinen looked at up her, his smile gone. He seemed uncertain now. 'It's a beautiful song.'

'Yes,' Kirsti agreed. 'All about the village welcoming the new bride with the new moon. A happy story, love and marriage. I hope it doesn't make you cry.' She grinned at him. 'Go on, you two, play.'

Anni bent over her instrument and the plaintive notes rang out. Kirsti closed her eyes and let the music flow over her skin. Her daughter was no one's fool, there was no doubt about that. Kirsti was hardly surprised when she opened her eyes at the end of the tune to see that Väinämöinen had disappeared and her daughter did not even seem to notice.

'Play me another song, Anni,' Kirsti coaxed. Her child complied with another old runo tune that echoed across the room and the ages. As the notes reverberated, Kirsti knew she need not fear how her daughter knew this one.

'Lumottu' means 'enchanted.' While riding on the boat across Finland's Saimaa Lake to see the ancient rock paintings, I suddenly had a vision of a young girl telling a story about the northern witch Louhi on an empty stage, while Louhi herself danced behind her. By the time I got back to shore, I had a story in my head about an immigrant family who still found a great deal of magic in the old stories of the Kalevala, although their daughter (naturally enough) found it easier to see Louhi's point of view than that of the goddess' frequent opponent, Väinämöinen. Myth resonates deeply in some people; I guess I'm one of them.

LUMOTTU

Characters

MIKA   Father
LARA   Mother
LAURI   14 year-old Son
ARJA   12 year-old Daughter
MATTI   10 year-old Son
EMMI   7 year-old Daughter

LOUHI   Witch of the north, visible only to ARJA
GRANDMOTHER   LARA's mother (*part to be doubled with LOUHI*)

VÄINÄMÖINEN   Ancient rune singer
KARL   GRANDMOTHER's servant, about 50 yrs. old (*part to be doubled with VÄINÄMÖINEN*)

In Act 2

ADULT ARJA
ADULT MATTI

Setting

A farmhouse in Northern Michigan.

Time

ACT I: SCENE 1—Morning, spring 1912
         SCENE 2—Midday, the same
ACT II: SCENE 1—Afternoon, late fall 1932

Performance Note:

The songs sung by the characters in this play may be found in *Laulupiiri: Saestykset / Singing Circle: Accompaniments*, by Anja Sell. See page 169 below for more information on this songbook.

ACT I, SCENE 1

A farm house; early morning. All is dark.

*ARJA enters STAGE RIGHT with candle, walks to the
middle of the room and kneels, illuminated.*

ARJA
When the great smith, Ilmarinen, went north to seek the
hand of the beautiful maiden of Pohjola, Louhi Queen of
the North set many tasks before him. Many said they were
impossible.

*LOUHI enters from behind ARJA, raises arms costumed to
indicate eagle's wings.*

LOUHI
My daughter is no ordinary child, no farmer's daughter.
To win her hand you must prove a hero.

ARJA
He was asked to plough a field of serpents.

LOUHI
Ilmarinen forged a plow of silver and gold on the advice
of my fair girl, with that instrument he furrowed the field
well.

ARJA
He was asked to bring home the bear of Tuonela.

LOUHI
Ilmarinen forged a bridle of steel and iron on the advice
of my fair girl, with that headpiece he led home the bane of
the land of the dead.

ARJA
He was asked to catch the great pike without net or line.

LOUHI
Ilmarinen forged a bright eagle on the advice of my fair girl, with that bird he plucked the pike from Tuoni's black river.

ARJA
Louhi finally relinquished her daughter.

LOUHI
The wedding feast went on for days, the buckets of beer flowed, the salmon leaped upon the plates. Then Ilmarinen took the bride away, back to the southern lands of his birth.

ARJA
And yet within the year she died, died because she was far from home.

LOUHI withdraws, lights come up to reveal the rest of the family at work around the house.

LARA [*stirring porridge over the fire*]
I heard your grandmother's footfall when I awoke this morning.

ARJA
All the way across the valley from her house?

LARA
Indeed, and surely she will be here by dinner time. So step lively, children. You know how your grandmother hates a dusty home.

LAURI [*coming through the door with firewood*]
Pappi says there's much milk today, an extra pail at least.

LARA
Arja, Arja! What are you doing on the floor there? Go

out and bring the milk in. Why do you linger, girl? There's
much to be done.

MATTI [*grinding at a quern*]
Arja is dreaming again!

EMMI [*kneading dough at the table*]
Dreamer, dreamer, Arja is a dreamer!

LARA
Hush, child! Arja, go please. Now.

ARJA exits.

Is there enough salmon, Lauri? Did you check the
smokehouse?

LAURI [*arranging firewood by the fire*]
Yes, Mammi. There's plenty, enough for six grandmoth-
ers! Not that Mummo eats all that much. She hardly eats as
much as a sparrow.

LARA [*laughs*]
No mind; it is not how much a guest eats, but how
much she is offered.

MATTI
What if she eats everything?

EMMI
Everything?!
LARA
Then we would have to go without, my selfish boy. You
will have to remember, when you are a man yourself, to
always greet guests with comfort and generosity, however
unwelcome they may be. For the worst guests judge you
harshly.

MATTI
Then I shall have no guests ever and keep everything to
myself.

EMMI
Well, I won't visit you then. You're so mean!

MATTI
Good! I won't invite you.

MATTI sticks out tongue at EMMI.

LARA
Children, don't quarrel. You know what Grandmother
says.

LAURI
'A magpie will come along and take your tongue!'

MATTI
There aren't any magpies here. Pappi says so.

LAURI
I'm sure a blue jay will do as well. Look—there's one at
the window now. Better hide, Matti!

*Amidst general laughter, ARJA and MIKA enter, he with
two pails, she with one. As the scene progresses, MIKA pours
milk into a churn, and ANJA places her pail by the fire to
warm.*

MIKA
It is good to hear the house ring with laughter, provided
duties are being attended to as well.

LARA
Always that caveat, as the pastor would require. Are we
not all well employed, children?

ALL
Yes, Mammi. Yes, Pappi.

LARA

There, you see? All at work, no idle hands. They know
their grandmother is on her way and want to make the
house welcoming for her.

MIKA

You northern women and your magical ways. Take care
Pastor Lindkvist doesn't decide to curse you for a heathen
spirit.

LARA

Pooh—Pastor Lindkvist takes not the slightest notice of
what women do, provided there is a glass of beer in front of
him and some good brown bread with butter. Or better yet,
a slab of pork.

MATTI

Or a piece of cake!

MIKA

Now see, wife, you have fomented revolution. Our son
shows no respect for the pastor of our village.

ARJA

Neither do your daughters, Pappi. I don't like Pastor
Lindkvist and his scowling face.

MIKA

He scowls, my girl, because he must face obdurate
parishioners like my family members all day and try to
point them toward the narrow road of righteousness.

ARJA

What if I don't wish to go on that path?

MIKA

Now don't say that, child. I plan to see you in heaven
when we receive our everlasting glory.

MIKA pauses to lay a hand on ARJA's shoulder.

You will play the kantele for your grandmother when she
comes?

ARJA
Yes, Pappi.

MIKA
She always says that no one plays it as sweetly as you do.

ARJA
Like the spirit of Tapio's forest, she says, like Ilmatar's
breath.

MIKA
Like an angel, that would be better to say. The woods are
God's provenance, so to the air that we breathe. Now, to
your churning, young lady.

LARA [*singing*]
'Who is going to heat the sauna?'

MIKA
Well, let's see: The firewood is brought in, the milk is in
the churn, and the flour is ground.

MATTI [*quietly*]
Almost.

MIKA
Well, my men. Shall we heat the sauna, gather the birch
twigs and take the first turn ourselves?

LAURI
Yes, do let's. I think we have been working hard and
deserve it.

MIKA
Hard work is its own reward.

ALL
As Pastor Lindkvist says.

MIKA

Rather than scold your impertinence, I will commend
you on a lesson well learned. Lauri, why don't you get the
birch twigs. And Matti, you get some water in the bucket.

MATTI

But the water's so heavy, can't Lauri do it?

LAURI

I can do it, Pappi.

MIKA

Matti is capable, if he puts his mind to it. It won't do to
let such a lazybones whine his way out of his duty. Am I
right, son?

MATTI

Yes, Pappi.

*The three leave. ARJA goes to the churn and begins to work.
LARA pulls some herbs from the dried gatherings that hang
from the roof beam. EMMI moves over to the quern.*

EMMI

Ugh! Matti has not ground the grain enough, again. He
is such a lazybones.

LARA

Do me a favor, my sweet, and grind it as it ought be
done.

ARJA

Matti is such a lazybones. One day he will fall asleep in
the forest and never awaken, just like Antero Vipunen.

EMMI

Who is Antero Vipunen?

ARJA

He was a giant who fell asleep, and the great sage
Väinämöinen walked right into his stomach and built a fire
and demanded all the spells and the cures the giant knew

before he would extinguish the fire and finally leave, but by
then Väinämöinen had all the magic he would need.

 EMMI
Can we hear that story?!
LARA
I think we just did.

ARJA
Can we hear the story of Louhi as the eagle?

EMMI
You always want to hear Louhi stories. I want to hear
Aino's story, it's so sad.
ARJA
But Grandmother tells the Aino story so well. Please,
Mammi, tell us a Louhi story.

LARA
Naughty girl! You know that your grandmother will tell
you another Louhi story no doubt when she arrives.

ARJA
She will be tired from her long journey, there will probably be no time for a story tonight. Instead I will play the
kantele for her and sing Aino's sad lament and the cuckoo
song. We can sing it, Emmi and I.

LARA
All right, Emmi?

EMMI
Yes, Mammi. I want to sing for grandmother, too.

LARA
Very well. Now let's see, where to begin?

ARJA
Begin with the journey north, but after Väinämöinen
creates the pikebone kantele.

LARA
Yes, mistress Arja.

*While LARA tells the tale, the lights come down and
LOUHI appears behind her once more as she had with ARJA
earlier, echoing the events of the story in her movements.
Throughout, LARA stirs the porridge, EMMI makes the rolls,
and ARJA churns.*

When Väinämöinen, wise old magician of the Kalevala,
heard how the Sampo, the magic mill, milled every day
grain, salt and gold and brought such prosperity to the
people of the North, he decided that his folk, the people of
Kaleva in the South, must have the mill for themselves.

ARJA
It's wrong, isn't it, Mammi? They shouldn't take what
isn't theirs.

EMMI
Let Mammi tell the story, Arja!

LARA
Steadfast old Väinämöinen knew his people would
prosper if they had the Sampo, so he got together with
the handy smith Ilmarinen and the wayward hero
Lemminkäinen, and they stole away to the North.

ARJA
Where you used to live, before you came to Michigan?

LARA
Indeed. When they got there, they begged Louhi, wild
witch of the North, to share the Sampo with them, to share
its riches with the people of Kaleva. But Louhi refused.

EMMI
That wasn't nice.
ARJA
Väinämöinen had given the Sampo as a bridal gift for
her daughter's hand. Ilmarinen forged it for his wife, the

daughter who died when she was taken from her home.
Isn't that true, Mammi?

LARA
It is indeed true.

ARJA
And gifts once given should not be taken back.

EMMI
They only wanted to share.

ARJA
One shouldn't have to share one's own things, one's best.

LARA
Spoken like a middle child, my dear. Now let me go on:
When Louhi refused to part with the Sampo, Väinämöinen
brought out the pikebone kantele. He plucked its strings—

ARJA
Which were made of hairs from the tail of the ogre
Hiisi's gelding.

LARA
And he played a song so sweet and mournful that the
people of the North fell into a deep sleep, even Louhi.
Väinämöinen charmed their eyes to remain closed and their
lungs to breathe deeply and slowly. Then the three heroes
went to the copper mountain, which held the Sampo, the
magic mill.

ARJA
But there were ten locks on the door!

LARA
Ten locks! But this did not stop wise old Väinämöinen.
He told the handy smith Ilmarinen to oil the locks well
with butter so they did not squeak, and then Väinämöinen
sang them open with his magic song. Then with the help

of the great hero, Lemminkäinen, they got the Sampo onto
their boat and sailed away toward Kaleva.

EMMI
How did a magic song open locks?

ARJA
It's magic, that's how.

EMMI
But how?

LARA
Väinämöinen knew the secret origin of all elements,
of iron and steel, of wind and rain. When you know the
secrets of a thing, you can control it. But you must know its
true name and you must comprehend its true nature. That
knowledge is power.

LARA pauses to see whether this has settled the debate.

The three men sailed away, but on the third day
Lemminkäinen could not stand the silence of the waves
any longer. 'Sing us a song, steadfast old Väinämöinen,' he
cried, 'Sing us a song to entertain us.'

ARJA
Which was a mistake!

LARA
Indeed it was, which Väinämöinen knew. He refused
the request and tried to hush the wayward hero, but
Lemminkäinen kept insisting, 'We must have a song, and if
you won't sing, I will!' He opened his throat and out burst a
song that was not in the lovely tones of the rune singer but
a wild squawk of a melody, and it woke a nearby crane from
a sound slumber and she flew away to the North, squawk-
ing the same discordant melody.

ARJA
And Louhi awoke from her long slumber!

LARA

And was she ever angry when she saw the ten locks
standing open and the copper mountain empty. She
knew that the Kaleva men had stolen the Sampo, and she
gathered her own war-like men on a giant ship and headed
south for a battle.

ARJA

But first!

LARA

Ah yes, I had nearly forgotten. First she sent the
mist-daughter to keep the Kaleva men's boat from moving,
sent the great sea serpent to upend the craft, and sent the
mighty wind and waves to take them to a watery grave.

ARJA

But all in vain.

LARA

Keep churning, Arja. We must have fresh butter for
your grandmother's bread. Yes, all in vain. Steadfast old
Väinämöinen brought forth his charmed blade, waved it
through the mist, and the mist-daughter departed. The
great sea serpent menaced the heroes' boat and frightened
poor Ilmarinen, but old Väinämöinen grabbed the serpent
by the ears until he whimpered and promised never to
trouble men again.

ARJA

Which is why there are no sea serpents today.

LARA

There are, however, strong winds and waves, and even
old Väinämöinen had trouble with them. The winds blew
so fiercely that the great pikebone kantele—

ALL

Fell into the sea and was lost forever.

LARA

Which made steady old Väinämöinen quite sad and he lamented the loss loudly. He called on the water gods, Ahto and Ahti, asked them for safe passage upon the waters, and the wayward hero Lemminkäinen strengthened the sides of the boat as much as possible, but still Louhi's ship was gaining fast and would soon catch the thieves. Steadfast wise old Väinämöinen had a plan, however. He took a small flint from his pocket and threw it into the waves. The wise old rune singer sang a charm which turned the flint into a reef and in no time Louhi's ship crashed upon it and broke into a thousand pieces.

ARJA
But that did not stop the queen of the North who was wise and strong.

EMMI
She was evil!

ARJA
She was not.

EMMI
Was too!

ARJA
Was not—she was wise and powerful, was she not, Mammi?

LARA
She was indeed. The men of Kaleva thought her evil because she had what they wanted. The people of the North thought the men of Kaleva were evil because they took her treasure away.

EMMI
Pastor Lindkvist says that we must always flee evil.

LARA
Indeed we should: evil makes the spirit heavy.

EMMI

But if the people of the North thought the people of
South were evil and the people of the South thought those in
the north were evil, who was right?

ARJA

They should have shared.

LARA

There is your answer, Emmi. Judgment—we are given
wisdom to choose the right path, to do the least harm, with
the knowledge that it is not possible to pass through this
world without causing some harm. Weigh your choices,
consider the needs of others, see the hawk's eye view, not
your own selfish desires. Unless you live alone like a bear in
the woods, you must always think of others when you make
your decisions.

EMMI

The pastor makes it sound much more simple.

LARA

He is a simple man.

ARJA

Don't stop, Mammi, just when we get to the best part!

LARA

Ah yes, the best part, of course. The queen of the North
took the remnants of the ship, old rakes and hoes and turned
herself into a giant eagle.

ARJA

With sharp claws and a beak of iron and wings as wide as
a mountain.

LARA

She had a hundred men under her wing and a thousand
under her tail feathers. Louhi flew across the waves right
to the heroes' boat. 'Give me the Sampo,' she demanded.
'Never!' cried Väinämöinen. The two of them struggled so

long and so very hard, but finally the Sampo dropped into
the waves.

ARJA
And broke into a thousand pieces.

LARA
And broke into a thousand pieces. Some lay in the
ocean, some bounced into the sky and some washed up on
the shores of Finland and made the land rich forever more.

LOUHI withdraws once more into darkness.

ARJA
Mammi, then why did you and Pappi leave Finland to
come to this land? Did a piece of the Sampo wash up here?

LARA
I think it must have, for this is a green and pleasant land
with deep forests and laughing rivers and a broad blue sky.
The bear walks here, too, and the pike swims in the great
deep lake.

ARJA
But there is no magic.

LARA
There is always magic—but those who do not have the
eye to see it seldom find it. It was always thus.

EMMI
Magic like talking birds?

LARA
Your grandmother understands the languages of the
birds.

ARJA
That is not the same.

LARA

Is it not? Do you understand Pastor Lindkvist when he
speaks to his mother in his own tongue?

ARJA *and* EMMI

No.

LARA

There you are.

ARJA

But he learned it from his mother, I guess. That's not
magic.

LARA

And who taught your grandmother the language of
birds? It is not a thing which she learned at her mother's
knee. Magic is not always big and noisy. Often it is simple
and homely. But like the blue jays, we like shiny things.
What is familiar is never valued as much as something
novel. We overlook the magic under our noses.

Sounds indicate the return of the others.

Here is your father and the boys. Shall we to the sauna,
my girls?

ARJA

Matti must finish the churning, for I have not done
enough. I'm sorry, Mammi.

*The door opens to admit MIKA, MATTI, and LAURI, who
wear only their trousers and are sweaty, with towels variously
draped about them.*

MIKA

Who's ready for the sauna? It's quite hot now, and
afterwards the snow feels great.

LAURI
I took the top seat and stayed there longer even than
Pappi, did I not?

MIKA
And he dumped a bucket of water straight from the
spring right over his head immediately after. Quite a young
man we have here.

MATTI [*sidling over toward ARJA*]
I rubbed snow all over my face.

MIKA
That you did. Two fine young men.

*MATTI slips some snow down ARJA's neck, making her
shriek and jump up.*

ARJA
Matti! You terrible boy.

MATTI laughs.

I wish I could become an eagle and drop you in a
swamp.

LARA
Now girls, let's hurry out to the sauna. Your grandmother
will be here soon and there's still so much to do. Matti,
churn the butter—now, no complaints, young man—Lauri,
don't let the cakes burn. Come girls, time to get clean.

Act I, Scene 2

Farmhouse, midday: the stage is dark at first.

ARJA is discovered CENTER STAGE with spotlight, folding napkins at the table.

ARJA
When Louhi was displeased by the cruelties of the people from the South, she stole the sun and the moon and all the fires went out.

LOUHI appears with eagle wings still, but with fire in one hand and the moon and sun projected behind her. As ARJA speaks, LOUHI follows with appropriate actions.

Louhi hid the moon in a mountain of steel and the sun in a mountain of iron. All over the world, people wondered what had happened to the lights in the sky and the flames in their kitchens. Väinämöinen cast lots made from the alder tree and discovered what she had done. He turned into a fish and headed to the Northland, but alone he could not undo the nine locks which kept the fortress fast.

He returned to the mighty smith, to Ilmarinen, to ask him to forge keys, ice picks and spears with which to open the mountain. Louhi flew south and perched outside the smithy. 'What do you forge there, man of steel?' the little bird asked him. Ilmarinen, who had hammered the arc of the sky, recognized Louhi and lied, 'I forge a great collar with which we will imprison the Queen of the North and chain her to the iron mountain, so she may never again steal the sun and the moon.'

Louhi grew afraid, for she loved freedom even more than she wanted revenge. The thought of being chained up fright-

ened her so much that she freed the sun and the moon from
the mountain stronghold, and fire returned to the world.

*LOUHI withdraws before the lights come up. The finishing
touches are being put around the farmhouse with all the family
except LAURI present.*

LARA
Are all the napkins in place, Arja? Is there enough
firewood, Mika? Emmi, is the last loaf ready to be sliced?

MIKA
Darling, all is ready. Arja has just put the last napkin in
its place. Matti has just brought another armful of wood
and Lauri will be back soon with your mother on his arm.

LARA
Everything should be perfect. Is the sauna still warm?
Mama will want a nice turn after her long walk here.

EMMI
Why did Mummo not take the wagon and have old Karl
drive her? It seems very odd. Such a long way.

LARA
You know how your grandmother is when she has made
up her mind.

MIKA check earlier
Immovable as Iron Mountain!

ARJA
I think I see them, yes! Just coming over the rise. Lauri
and—

ARJA stops, puzzled.

MIKA
And your grandmother, too, I presume. Your mother is
never wrong.

ARJA [*pause, then as normal*]
Yes, it is she. Hello, Mummo!

*She watches at the door for a moment, then steps back to
admit LAURI and GRANDMOTHER. Everyone but LARA
gathers to greet her warmly. LARA lingers by the fire until the
others have given their hugs and kisses.*

LARA [*walking up to put her hands on
GRANDMOTHER's shoulders*]
When was it?

GRANDMOTHER
Early this morning as I slept. Dear child.

LARA
Mama.

*She hugs GRANDMOTHER somewhat fiercely, then pulls
back to look at her, arms still on shoulders.*

Oh, Mama.

GRANDMOTHER
Now, no tears, my child. We shall be happy today. I am
surrounded by those I love and I am so very lucky.

MIKA [*somewhat puzzled*]
You would think you had not seen your mother in many
long years, my darling.

LARA [*wiping away tears*]
I am simply so very glad to have her with us today.

GRANDMOTHER [*patting LARA's cheek to comfort her*]
You are a good daughter, my Lara. And you have wonderful daughters yourself—and handsome sons.

ARJA
Mummo, Mammi—what is wrong?

MIKA

Arja, there is nothing wrong. Mammi and Grandmother
are just feeling rather sentimental today. Spring fever, that
is it.

LARA

Yes, Arja. Do not be troubled. Sometimes the sorrows of
the future have a way of intruding on the present.

MIKA

Sorrows?

LAURI

Mummo, the sauna is all ready for you. We have it as hot
as you like and there are plenty of whisks to get your blood
going. Pappi even has a little glass of schnapps ready for
you!

EMMI

I want schnapps!

LAURI

You're not having schnapps, Emmi. You're much too
young.

MIKA

Quite right. It will stunt your growth, Emmi, and you'll
stay as short as you are right now.

EMMI

Is that what happened to Mister Koskinen?

*ALL laugh. LARA and GRANDMOTHER use the
distraction for another desperate hug, parting after a moment.
Arja notices and keeps her eyes upon them during the following.
GRANDMOTHER sits, and the others gather around her.*

GRANDMOTHER

Thank you, Lauri, for the sauna preparations, but I think
I would rather wait. Perhaps in a bit, by and by. But right
now I want to sit with my grandchildren and hear their
news.

ARJA

We don't have news. Nothing ever happens around here.

GRANDMOTHER

I said it the day you were born: you have your grandfather's feet.

LARA

She will leave us and travel the world, just like my Pappi. Children, your isoisä was never happy unless there was a new road in front of him. It must have been hard for you, mama.

GRANDMOTHER

Ah, no. There were times when I wished he were home more, but I never got tired of hearing his steps turn back my way. There's such a thing as too much togetherness.

LARA

Mama!

GRANDMOTHER

Lara, you should know. I loved your father, but there was no need to put a bit in his mouth. If I had tried to keep him home, I would have lost him forever. You cannot pen something that needs to be free. Besides, when he returned I always knew that he did so because he loved me and wanted to be with me.

MIKA

I don't think I could ever leave my Lara.

He crosses to embrace LARA.

A day without her would be worse than the darkest day of winter.

GRANDMOTHER

Your heart needs to be near what it loves. My Matti's heart was a bird's heart, always soaring.

MATTI

I don't have to be like him just because I have his name,
do I, Mummo? I would rather have a big house and many
servants to work for me.

ARJA

You are just lazy, Matti.

MATTI

I'm not lazy; I'm resourceful.

GRANDMOTHER

You must remember to think as highly of others as your
do of yourself, my little one. Otherwise life gets lonely.

MATTI

Oh, when I am a rich man, I will let you all come live
with me and enjoy my fine house.

ALL laugh.

LARA

Mama, are you ready to eat? Or would you like to sit for
a little longer?

GRANDMOTHER

No, no—let us all sit and enjoy this meal together.
Come, sit, let us share.

*They sit around the table variously, ARJA on one side of her
GRANDMOTHER, LARA on the other.*

MIKA [*waving at MATTI's furtive grasp for some bread*]
Pastor Lindkvist would remind us of the importance of
thankfulness before we eat. Matti, why don't you say grace?

MATTI

For that which we are about to receive let us prove very
grateful. Amen!

He reaches for the bread.

Mummo, would you like a nice slice of bread? See,
Pappi, it was not for myself that I reached. For Mummo.

MIKA
Very thoughtful, indeed.

GRANDMOTHER
Thank you, child.

LARA
Stew for you, mama.

GRANDMOTHER
Just a little, dear. I do not have the appetite I once did.

LARA reacts to this.

GRANDMOTHER
Now, dear. Don't let it worry you.

LARA
Mama…

GRANDMOTHER
Hush, now. Emmi, how are you doing at your spelling?
And reading?

EMMI
I can spell almost everything! Miss Laitinen says my
work is excellent.

MIKA
She is always at the head of her class, which is more than
I can say for the rest of my children.

LAURI

I am ready to be out in the world working. I don't want
to read about life. I want to live it.

ARJA
I like to read history and myths and other stories.

MATTI
Arja is a daydreamer. She cannot keep her mind in this
world.

ARJA
At least I know my multiplication tables, too.

LARA
Children, don't bicker. It is a special day for your grandmother. I want today to be, to be…perfect.

GRANDMOTHER
Lara, fear not. The day will be perfect.

LARA
Oh, mama! [*She begins to cry.*]

GRANDMOTHER
There now, child, hush. All will be will. Everything is as
it should be.

ARJA
There is something wrong that you are not telling us,
Mummo.

MIKA
Arja, don't be silly. Your grandmother simply wants to
have everyone in harmony for her visit. Be good to one
another, all right?

ALL CHILDREN
Yes, Pappi.

GRANDMOTHER
Mika, do not worry. It is a joy to be surrounded by those

I love. My husband is nearby today, too, I can feel him. All is well.

MIKA
Lara, do not cry.

LARA
They are tears of joy, my sweet.

ARJA
Mammi, I don't understand. Why is everything so strange today? Why is Mummo so sad?

LARA
You heard your grandmother, she is not sad. She is joyful. Now, eat your dinner and listen to your Mummo.

GRANDMOTHER
Child, you have many great gifts. Let me tell you a story.
EMMI
Yay! A story.

MATTI
Tell 'Hannus Pannus'! No, tell 'Palakainen.'

ARJA
No, no—tell a tale of Louhi!

EMMI
But you already had Mammi tell the Louhi story! Tell something else.

GRANDMOTHER
This is the story of the bear hunt—

ARJA
Oh!

LARA
Never mind, Arja. There will be time later for other tales.

GRANDMOTHER
This is the story of the bear hunt.

MATTI
A boy's story!

GRANDMOTHER
A story for everyone—we all need to understand respect.
Shall I begin?

ALL
Yes, please Mummo!

GRANDMOTHER
The hunter puts on his snowshoes, on the day the first
snow falls. The fine flakes drift down and he knows it is
time.

*As GRANDMOTHER speaks, LAURI moves over to mime
the story with actions much like the Louhi sequences earlier.*

He calls to Beastie, his trusty dog, and together they
head into Tapio's realm. The pine scent is crisp and the
morning light soft. The white blanket muffles the sound of
his footsteps. Their steps are the first in the snow. No rabbit
has passed this way, no vole padding between bushes.

As he walks, he calls out to Tapio, 'I am one of your
men, Tapio, I am a fellow of the forest. Guide my arrows
on this special day, my bow made of your sapling's strength.
Grant me the gift that I seek this day that my family may
eat, that our winter be soft.

'Lead my step in the right direction, lead me to where
the honey-paw feeds. Let this poor man find his way
through the firs, let the birches show the path. Greenbeard,
direct my steps down the silver lanes and across the barren
rocks to where the great one turns his slowing steps. May
our feast be grand tonight.

'Tellervo, mother of the woodlands, keep me safe from
Otso's jaws. See that his claws do not injure. Welcome will he
be at our feasting, honored at the table's head.'

His snowshoes pace onward toward the ridge where the
den of the honeyed one lies, among the brambles and the
berry bushes. There he finds the long hair, sees the iron-jawed
one.

MIKA performs as a bear.

Strong and true his arrow, swift and clean the aim. With
his faithful companion beside him, the hunter returns to the
family table, the stout old traveler upon his shoulders. Joyful
was that day's reunion, grateful were the folk that day. Otso
joined the happy feasting, seated at the table's head.

Then the wise one speaks his thoughts, offers up his gratitude. 'Thank you, gentle honey paw, thank you, gold-furred
friend! Now our mouths will share your feast, now our bellies
filled and warm.'

Where does Otso come from? He comes from the stars in
the sky, where he returns at the end of the feast. We share his
flesh between us, and his gifts as well. The head of the honey
paw brings wisdom. His teeth make us fierce. His nose makes
us smell out trouble. His eyes offer foresight of events yet
to occur. His tongue gives us the poetry of the woods. His
golden fur keeps us warm. The king of Tapio's forest brings
us honor and plenty. Long may he roam from forest to sky.
To Otso, the honey paw!

ALL raise their glasses and drink.

ARJA
Thank you, Mummo. I will tell the bear story, too, one
day.

GRANDMOTHER
That is your gift, Arja.

LAURI

And I shall hunt the great one in his lair one day and
bring the bounty home.

GRANDMOTHER

And that is your gift, Lauri.

MATTI

What is my gift, Mummo?

GRANDMOTHER

Your gift will be a surprise, even to you, Matti.

MATTI

I hope it is very valuable.

GRANDMOTHER

It will be.

LARA

Mama, can I get you anything else? You have hardly
touched your stew.

GRANDMOTHER

No, Lara, my sweet. I am not that hungry. And it is
getting late. I shall have to go to the sauna soon.

LARA

So soon?

GRANDMOTHER

It has been a lovely visit, a lovely meal. So good to be
with you all and to hear my Matti's steps nearby.

LARA

But we must have a song or two first, surely?

GRANDMOTHER

Perhaps one song together and then I must go out.

LARA
Arja, take down the kantele and play for us.

MIKA
What shall we sing? How about 'The Spinster'!

LAURI
Pappi, it's bad luck to sing that song with unmarried
women in the house.

EMMI
Pappi, let's sing 'Nyt nouskaa lapsikullat!' That's a happy
one.

*ALL sing as ARJA strums. After a pause, ARJA begins
another tune, 'Vaka vanha Väinämöinen, laulaja iänikuinen.'*

ARJA [*playing the opening of the song on her kantele, and
singing*]
Vaka vanha Väinämöinen, laulaja iänikuinen—

*ALL join the song and sing three verses. VÄINÄMÖINEN
enters and puts his hands on GRANDMOTHER's shoulders.
She places her hands on his looking up at him, and at the
end of the song she rises. VÄINÄMÖINEN remains standing
behind her.*

GRANDMOTHER
One last song before I go—

LARA
Not yet! Just another bite first.

GRANDMOTHER
No, Lara, my child. Just one final song. Listen well, Arja.
Your mother will help you remember this song: [*sings*]
Noita laulan, joita tiijän, joita tiijän ja tajuan,
Noita laulan, joita tiijän, joita tiijän ja tajuan,
Noita ennen eukko neuvoi, oma vanhempi opetti,
Kultaisilla kunnahilta, metisillä mättähillä.

Noita laulan, joita tiijän, joita tiijän ja tajuan, noita laulan.

And now I must go to the sauna. Arja and Emmi, will you sing me 'Kylä vuotti uutta kuuta' as I go out? The beautiful tune will lighten my heart.

ARJA
Yes, Mummo. Of course.

LARA clasps GRANDMOTHER close while the others look on somewhat puzzled. ARJA plucks a few notes absently, her eyes riveted on her mother and grandmother.

MATTI [*slightly uncomfortably*]
Mummo, here. Take the finest towel for your sauna. Mammi and Arja worked for weeks on the embroidery. See? It has lovely birch trees and birds.

GRANDMOTHER
Kiitos, Matti. You are very kind. Now sing, girls. Be well, all of you. I love you all.

ALL
We love you, too, Mummo!

ARJA and EMMI begin to sing. LARA lets go of her mother. GRANDMOTHER walks slowly to the door, towel over her arm, with VÄINÄMÖINEN shadowing her. At the threshold she turns to take one more look, then steps outside with VÄINÄMÖINEN following. The door closes. LARA turns away and sits down heavily at the table. The song comes to its natural conclusion.

ARJA
Mammi, why are you so sad?

LARA
Loss is an inevitable part of life, my child. It is the worst part of love, too, and gives love its sweetness. But the loss is no easier to bear for all that.

MIKA *[reaching to comfort his wife]*
Darling, why so sad when your mother is here? You
should be happy.

LARA
Yes, dear. I know. I know.

MIKA
Arja, sing us another song, a happy one of joy and
celebration.

*LARA sobs, MIKA looks confused. A knock comes at the
door.*

Lauri, will you see who that is?

*LAURI crosses the room and opens the door to reveal KARL,
hat clutched in his hand.*

KARL
Good afternoon, everyone. Mister Mika, Miss Lara,
children.

MIKA
Karl, good to see you. Sit, eat—there is plenty yet.

LAURI
Karl, I hope you brought the cart. I cannot believe
Mummo walked all the way here this morning.

KARL
Walked? What?

MIKA
Karl, please, sit! Why do you stand there?

KARL
I bring news. I bring sad news.

MIKA
What is it, Karl? Out with it.

KARL
I don't know how to say, but to simply say it. Your
mother is dead, Miss Lara.

*LARA does not react, but ARJA runs to her side and
embraces her; MIKA gives a surprised bark of laughter.*

MIKA
Don't be ridiculous, Karl. She is out in the sauna even
now. What could make you say such a thing?

KARL
Out in…the sauna?

MIKA
Yes, she just went out to take her sauna a few minutes
ago. Lauri, run out and tell your grandmother that Karl is
here.

LAURI exits through the door.

Karl, what on earth were you thinking?

KARL
I know what I know.

MIKA
We will see in a moment. Look, you have made Lara cry.

KARL
Miss, I am so sorry. I do not wish to make you cry.

LARA
It is all right, Karl. It is not your fault. Someone has to
bear bad news, if not you, it would have been the rabbit or
the grouse or the tiny field mouse. Best it was from her own
lips I learned it.

ARJA
Mammi, I don't understand.

LARA
Your grandmother is dead.

MIKA
Lara, no—it is all a misunderstanding. You'll see.

*LAURI returns, opening the door slowly, the towel in his
hands.*

LAURI
She wasn't there. Just her towel.

KARL
I told you.

MIKA
Don't be foolish. She was right here. She ate with us…

LARA
It's all right, Mika. Karl is right. My mother is dead.

*The other children join ARJA around LARA, weeping and
consoling one another equally.*

MIKA
But she was here! I spoke with her, I saw her—she ate
food with us!

LARA
She wanted to say good-bye. It was so kind of her to
come.

MIKA
But—

*MIKA stands irresolutely for a moment, then slowly walks
over to the rest of the family and joins their embrace.*

ACT II

Interior of the farmhouse; very differently dressed overall, but with some familiar elements such as the table. There is a new door that allows entry from the side.

ARJA is discovered sitting at the table, lit cigarette in her hand, coffee cup as ashtray. She's dressed in stylish blouse and trousers, with a hat on the table and luggage piled next to the table. As ARJA speaks, LARA appears in the background with a rake to mime the story.

ARJA

When the hero Lemminkäinen died upon Tuonela's dark river, his mother wept upon the shore and called for a rake forged by the great smith, Ilmarinen. She begged the sun to burn so hot that the watchers of the shore, the people of Mana, would grow listless, fall into slumber.

Then the mother swept the rake through the black waters of Tuonela, found here a toe, here a finger, found a shirt and stockings, too. But all she had were parts, not a whole. So she called upon the lady in the air whose spindle knits the very sky, said, 'Come, o come where you are needed, come and bind his veins once more.' Flesh to flesh Lemminkäinen was joined once more, but he could not speak, so she called to the little bee to bring sweet honey from the meadow for his lips. Then it flew beyond the stars and returned with a nectar even greater than honey.

From this nectar the mother made an ointment, anointed every broken joint, healed with care the broken bones, rubbed the flesh to newborn pinkness. Then she spoke the charm of waking, pulled him from the sleep of death.

MATTI [*entering from the side door*]
Arja, you're not leaving already!

ARJA
I really have to be going if I'm going to get down to
Detroit for my flight back.

MATTI
But you just got here! You can't just come for the funeral
and then leave. What will people say?

ARJA
You know I don't much care what people say, Matti.

MATTI
That's one thing that will never change. I can't believe
you wanted to stay out here. It's so drafty in this room this
time of year.

ARJA
It's hard to believe we grew up in this tiny place.

MATTI
Not for me. I still see it every day. Maybe it's hard for
you because you haven't seen it in so many years. Lauri
comes back more than you do, and he's in Minnesota. He
rides the rails and gets here regularly. I hope when things
are better he will be able to bring Anya and little Lara.

ARJA
Things are not going to be getting better any time soon.

MATTI
Is this the reporter speaking? Are you sharing inside
information?

ARJA
I'm just saying what no one wants to admit. Things are
not getting better, they're getting worse. Look at what's
happening all over: the famine in the Soviet Union, the

militants in Germany and Switzerland. And right here, too.
Tell me you were not shocked when the police killed those
people at the Ford plant in Dearborn!

MATTI
They were agitators, I heard.

ARJA
They were people who wanted their jobs back. Even the
farmers revolted this summer, out in Oklahoma and Kansas!

MATTI
There are always bad seasons. We lay by what we can and
hope for better luck next year. It's best not to be too greedy.
Most of us can get by on what we have if we are careful and
thrifty.

ARJA [*laughs*]
I cannot believe you are saying that.

MATTI
You used to know what farm life was like.

ARJA
No, I mean you, always so lazy, always wanting to find
someone else to finish your work. You had such dreams of
wealth and riches, the easy life.

MATTI
Things are different, things have been different since you
left. Mammi and Pappi were struggling while you were off
with Amelia Earhart and Hattie Caraway. Women seem to
want to do anything except stay at home these days.

ARJA
I can see why you have not yet married. Such a charmer
for the ladies.

MATTI
I have been too busy. First there was Father's accident.
And about the time he recovered—

ARJA

Then it was the influenza. I know. It must have been
horrible for you.

MATTI

I was too busy to even consider it, but you're right. It has
been horrible. The Sippolas, the Lindstroms, the Mäkinens—
everyone lost at least one of the family.

ARJA

The 'flu has killed many across the borderlands. People
like to say that it came down from Canada, but there's little
to support such a theory. Poor health and poorer nutrition
are the most likely culprits. In the city, it spreads so quickly.

MATTI

It spreads quickly here, too, on market day, at church.
People aren't willing to stay home when they feel it coming
on. Think it's just a cold.

ARJA

Did you get sick at all?

MATTI

I was ill for a while, before Mammi got very bad. Pappi
was very weak. I was getting better when Mammi fell ill.
In the end they died within a day of each other, Pappi then
Mammi. It's good that the frost has not come yet.

ARJA

Matti, don't be so gruesome.

MATTI

It's not gruesome, it is simply what must be done.

ARJA

I cannot get accustomed to how you have changed. Selfish
little Matti has become a thoughtful and responsible man.

MATTI

There was little other option. Lauri had gone to Illinois to find work when the lumberyard here first began to lay off crews. There was no one left to care for Mammi and Pappi.

ARJA

I know, I am sorry. If I could have gotten away—

MATTI

Yes, yes. I know. Your life is far from here. The swirl of the international press.

ARJA

It's not as exciting as it sounds. I spend most of my time in a smoky office full of men who drink too much and swear. I hardly even see my apartment until I'm ready to collapse at the end of the day.

MATTI

Ah, but how many times have you been to Paris and to London?

ARJA

Ha! What do I see in Paris? Same thing I see in London: another office, a tiny hotel room, and, if I'm lucky, a greasy restaurant where politicians eat.

MATTI

But never to Finland yet.

ARJA

I tried to get an assignment to go interview the People's Party founders, but the head office didn't think it was sufficiently newsworthy.

MATTI

A country too small to matter, a language too hard to learn; one day the Soviets will simply swallow Finland and no one will care.

ARJA

Now don't say that. You would be surprised how people
will rally around the underdog. Besides, all Finns have
plenty of *sisu*. When things are worst, we are at our best.

MATTI

It's a romantic notion. But I didn't feel so full of *sisu*
when I was nursing our parents and running the whole
farm.

ARJA

I imagine not. If I could have come back…

MATTI

Yes, yes, so you say.

ARJA

I'm lucky to have a job, Matti. I want to be able to keep
it. There's a Depression on, you know.

MATTI

I'm well aware of it. Up here no one has more than a
couple of nickels to rub together. You have no idea how
people suffer. In the midst of all the sickness, there was only
Doctor Hastrup and he became ill, too. Then there was no
one but old Miss Laitinen with her strange cures and snake
fat.

ARJA

I had forgotten! But Mummo had the same cures, the
same old rhymes. They worked, more often than not they
did work.

MATTI

You were always her favorite. Didn't she pass a lot of
those songs and cures on to you? You were always reciting
the old stories, singing the old runos.

ARJA

I can still remember them, most of them. The Louhi

stories were always my favorites. She seemed invulnerable. I wanted to have her wings, her claws.

MATTI
Reading your columns, it would seem like you have.

ARJA
Now you are being unkind!

MATTI
Not at all. It's like you always said: good and bad depends entirely upon your point of view. It's good that you give those crooks the hard look.

ARJA
Sometimes I wish I could leave it all behind. The long hours, the endless deadlines, the bad food, the worse company. I sometimes think of coming back here and just living the simple way I used to do.

MATTI
Marry, settle down with some 'simple' farmer…

ARJA
Why not? It could happen. Like Mammi and Pappi, a perfect union of northern mysteries and southern can-do.

MATTI [*laughs*]
You're such a fool!

ARJA
What do you mean?

MATTI
The idea that you would be happy here! You couldn't wait to leave. You were practically running out the door every day since you could walk. If you were stuck here, you'd be miserable. It's just a pleasant fantasy that you can have for five minutes before you walk out the door yet again.

ARJA
That's not true.

MATTI
Of course it is. You can barely get here in time for the
funeral of our parents and now you're already leaving. So
don't lie to me and pretend that you want to stay.

ARJA
I'm sorry, Matti. I didn't know that I had made you so
angry.

MATTI
You never think about anyone but yourself. Why should
that be any different now, just because our parents are gone?

ARJA
Matti, you're being unfair. I just chose a different path
than you.

MATTI
'Chose!' What choice did I have? I never had any option
but to stay here and help. Don't you think I would have
liked to have had options?

ARJA
But I thought you were so happy here! I know things
have been difficult, things have been trying all over, it's a
Depression. We are all struggling. You would find my little
flat a miserable hole, that's why I don't spend much of any
time there. New York can be a real cesspool—

MATTI
I wouldn't know! I have never been south of Muskegon, I
have never even been to Chicago, let alone New York.

ARJA
Come to New York! Come with me. You are free now,
you can do as you like.

MATTI
You don't understand.

ARJA
I know, you had obligations. You have been dutiful, you have been the good one. But now you can change all that.

MATTI
No, you don't understand at all.

ARJA
What don't I understand?

MATTI
You make it sound as if I have been trapped here.

ARJA
Isn't that just what you have been telling me?

MATTI
No, not at all. It's not like that.

ARJA
Then come to New York with me! The farm needs little enough this time of year. Surely you can take a little time away, see New York, visit the Statue of Liberty and the Empire State Building.

MATTI
No! I can't do it. You don't understand.

ARJA
Make me understand.

MATTI
It's—different now.

ARJA
You mean because Mammi and Pappi have gone?

MATTI
No, before that.

ARJA
You mean—

MATTI
Nothing has been the same since Emmi died.

ARJA
I know.

EMMI appears behind ARJA.

MATTI
No. That's just it. You don't know. You weren't here.

ARJA
I was in India! I couldn't possibly have gotten back in
time for the funeral.

MATTI
And afterward? When we were all grieving? When we
were all wondering what had happened, how our precious
little sister could have been viciously murdered like that?
Didn't you think we could have used you here, to comfort
us, to share the grief—I don't know! Maybe to use those
reporter skills to find her killer?

ARJA
They did find him eventually.

MATTI
Two years! Two years of wondering, fearing, hating and
grieving. Her body was buried, but our outrage was not.
Pappi grew so grey. Mammi could not smile, but wept every
day. You should have come.

ARJA

I didn't know how to face you all. By the time I got back
from India, two months had passed. I wrote many letters to
Mammi and Pappi, I thought—I thought that was a help.

MATTI

Having you here would have been better. I could not do
everything. Lauri could only stay for a while and then he
had to go back. He has a family of his own to care for. It's
not like us. We are unattached.

ARJA

You don't understand, I inherited Grandfather's feet. Like
Grandmother always said about me and isoisä. I can't help
that. I have to travel, it's an itch. I can't stay in one place for
long.

MATTI

So why did you not travel here? Mammi cried for you,
she wanted her other daughter here to hold in her arms.
Why didn't you come? Why didn't you care enough to
come?

ARJA

I cared! I care! I was just frightened.

MATTI

The globe-trotter was frightened?! He was just some
crazy old man, he wasn't going to kill you, too. God, you're
so selfish, it's always about you.

ARJA

I wasn't afraid of him. I was afraid of you all.

MATTI

That's stupid.

ARJA

No, it's not.

MATTI

We were angry that you did not come, but we would
have forgiven you as soon as you showed up on our doorstep. We are family. This is your home.

ARJA

No, it's not. That's what I was afraid of. That if I came
you would try to make me stay and I would not be able to
stay and you would hate me.

MATTI

Was it really better to simply stay away and make sure
you broke everyone's heart? You abandoned us.

ARJA

You are always in my heart. Wherever I go, you are
always in my heart.

MATTI

Do you think that matters? Do you really? Do you think
that mattered to Emmi, lying there, dying alone?

*EMMI moves behind MATTI, laying a hand on his
shoulder, patting.*

You're a dreamer, you've always been a dreamer and
nothing has changed. You would rather be traveling because
then you only have to deal with dreams and not people.

ARJA

Do you remember that day, the day Mummo came, the
day she died?

MATTI
What?

ARJA

The day Mummo died. She came to this house when she
was already dead.

MATTI

What? You're talking about a dream.

ARJA

You were here! I was here. We were all here. Mummo
came, had dinner with us, told us the story of the bear
hunt, sang songs. She sang 'Noita Laulan' for me to remember. I still do.

ARJA begins to sing 'Noita Laulan.'

MATTI

You're conflating two different days. She was dead. She
did not sing or come to lunch. You dream, you were always
dreaming. Miss Laitinen always wrote that on your semester
reports.

ARJA

No, it was real—it happened. I don't know why you
don't want to believe it.

MATTI

Oh, is this supposed to make it all right? You had a nice
dream of Mummo where everything was fine and she got to
say good-bye and so it's all alright. Well, that's not the way
it is. People die, they are gone. I have seen enough to know
that is the case. People, horses, dogs, cats, birds—all die,
all end as nothing but rotting corpses. Despite what Pastor
Lindkvist told us as children, death is indeed the end.

*EMMI hugs him as he finishes the speech, then slowly moves
back behind ARJA.*

ARJA

No, I know what I know. That day is singed on my
memory. It is the day I learned there was nothing to fear.
It was the day I knew I would take up the wanderer's life
for good. I know it was real. And it was not the last time,
either.

MATTI

You're lying. It's your imagination.

ARJA

It's not. Do you want me to tell you how I know?

MATTI

No, I don't. I don't want to hear your dreams, your imaginings. You are not a noita, you are not a witch or a seer. You're just my sister, my sister who makes up lies for a living.

ARJA

The day Emmi died, I knew. The cable did not reach me for days, I had moved on from Benares, further down the Ganges traveling by boat. But in my hotel room that night, Emmi came to me.

EMMI puts her hands on ARJA's shoulders, who crosses her arms to place her hands on EMMI's.
Her head was red with blood. She told me she had little time, but wanted to say good-bye and how much she would miss me, how much she loved me.

MATTI

Lies! You just wanted to assuage your conscience.

ARJA

I could hardly believe it! It had been so long since Mummo's death, I had doubted. But there was a holy man I met in Benares, who traveled in our party. I told him about it and he laughed at my questions. 'Of course it is real,' he told me. 'Do you not recognize your sister?' He was amazed that I would doubt, yet you are amazed that I would believe.

MATTI

You can say anything, tell any story to make you feel better. But I know it is not true. Your guilt is what's real.

ARJA

Do you know the truth about what happened to Emmi?

MATTI

Of course, so does everyone. It was in the papers. Old
Jasper, the foreman at the sawmill, he killed her and that
other little girl, and then two years later, he killed himself
with rat poison on the floor of the sawmill. He left a note
confessing to both.

ARJA

But he didn't tell where he left their hands, did he?

EMMI snatches her arms back.

MATTI [*after a long pause*]
No.

ARJA
I know where they are.

MATTI
No.

ARJA
Emmi told me that night, when she visited.

MATTI
No. It cannot be.

ARJA
Emmi wanted me to know. She said not to tell anyone,
that I would need to know for some distant day. For today.

MATTI
No.

ARJA
To give you hope.

MATTI
You're lying, you're lying to torment me.

ARJA [*rising to cross the stage and embrace MATTI*]
No, I am telling the truth, so you believe, so you know
that dreams are possible, so you know that death is not
the end, so you know that you will see Emmi again, and
Mammi and Pappi and Mummo.

EMMI joins her, embracing MATTI.

MATTI [*breaking down, sobbing throughout ARJA's
speech*]
Emmi! Emmi!

ARJA
Tomorrow we will go. We will go get the constable and
go to the sawmill. Under the floor boards, there is a box
made of pine. In it we will find four sets of little hands,
Emmi's among them.

MATTI
No, no, we cannot.

ARJA
Yes, we must.

MATTI
Why? Why would he do such a thing? Those poor little
girls! My poor Emmi!

ARJA [*holding one of EMMI's hands in hers*]
She told me that he thought they were evil. Their hands
were the source of that evil. He knew they wanted him to
do evil. Their hands beckoned him. Made him want to do
evil things. The only way to stop their evil was to get rid of
their hands and the impure thoughts.

MATTI
How could he think that? How could he be so evil to
one so sweet?

EMMI takes one of his hands in hers.

And two more girls besides! Two other girls from here?
How did no one miss them?

ARJA

One was the child of an indigent family that had been
riding the rails. The other was thought to have run away.
Her mother did not much care that she was gone. There
were eight children all together. The father drank too much
and beat her. She was relieved to have one less to deal with.

MATTI

That's so horrible. How can there be so much evil?

ARJA

There is also good.

MATTI

Not enough of it.

ARJA

Of course not.

MATTI

So, that is your answer? The world is an evil place?

ARJA

The world is not an evil place, not as Pastor Lindkvist
would have you believe anyway. The world is a complicated
place where one person's evil is another person's good. We
bemoan the evil, but we do not treasure the good as much
as we ought to do. That's why there always seems to be
more evil.

MATTI

I don't think that's right.

ARJA

It is what I have seen. It is not possible to travel through
this world without causing harm, however good your
intentions may be. That is the way of the world.

MATTI
That's horrible.

ARJA
It is simply what is. We are living creatures. We must consume and one day we must expire. Our lives in between are filled with pain, but also with much joy.

MATTI
Joy is fleeting; pain lingers, grief lingers.

ARJA
Joy is ever new, ever ready to be found. But you have to seek it out.

MATTI [*wiping his eyes*]
I don't know. It's been in very short supply lately.

ARJA
If we put Emmi to rest, will you not feel some sense of relief, if not actual joy?
MATTI
Yes.

ARJA [*kissing EMMI's other hand*]
Then that we will do tomorrow.

EMMI releases their hands and retreats into the shadows.

MATTI
Then you're staying?

ARJA
I can send a cable to my editor and tell him I'm working on a story here.

MATTI
Will he know you're lying?

ARJA

Who says I'm lying?
MATTI
Your lips are moving.
They both laugh.

ARJA
There are always stories in this house. I think it was built
out of them.

MATTI
Mummo's stories. I do remember that day. I do remem-
ber how she could hear isoisä's step days before he returned.
She would have Grandfather's favorite meal ready—

ARJA
Pasties—

ARJA *and* MATTI
With no rutabaga!

MATTI
I always wanted the easy way out, to live in luxury and
ease. Look at me now. A farmer with dirty hands and a bent
back.
ARJA
Does it help to know that at least you have food and
open fields? In the city, there are so many starving, living on
top of each other, breathing the same air. I have to get away
sometimes just to inhale.

MATTI
It's because you don't have a sauna. You know what
isoisä always said, '*Jos vesi, votkaa, ja sauna ei auta, on tauti
kuolemaksi.*'

ARJA
'If water, vodka and sauna do nothing, the condition is
mortal!' Hey, does that mean you're going to heat the sauna
for me?
ARJA begins to sing 'Kukapa sen saunan lämmittääpi. '

MATTI

I suppose it must be my chore today. At least there is
plenty of wood for the fire already. But you will have to
help chop potatoes for the pasties tonight.

ARJA

It's a deal.

MATTI [*rising*]

Thank you for staying. For telling me about Emmi.

ARJA

Anything for my brother.

*MATTI exits out the front door. After a moment, VÄINÄ-
MÖINEN comes in from the side, carrying the kantele. ARJA
and VÄINÄMÖINEN go to center stage. She lights a candle
and he plucks a few notes as she speaks.*

When it became clear to Väinämöinen that the old ways
were losing their strength in the modern world, he conjured
up a copper boat and stood steadfast against the ocean's
winds. The wise old man, eternal sage, knew that one day
he would return. Again he would bring his magic, build the
Sampo, fight the enemies of Kaleva. The day would come
that the folk would need a new moon, or for him to set a
new sun in the sky. He could not bear to live in a world
where his name was forgotten, all magic despised. One day
he would return. Just then, however, he stepped into his
copper boat and sailed away to the ends of time. But he left
behind the kantele, the strings of joy, the rapturous sound.

*VÄINÄMÖINEN hands the kantele to ARJA, who then
smiles. VÄINÄMÖINEN walks away into the darkness.*

We are never without the joy of music, never without the
hope of songs in our hearts. In the darkness of every night,
we heat the sauna, fill the table and sing our songs, for the
living and the dead.

ARJA blows out candle and walks into the dark.
CURTAIN.

New Additions

One of the first songs I learned to play on the kantele was *Karhunpeijaispolska*, 'The Bear Feast Polska' which I somehow imagined in a very sweet, storybook kind of way. Then I learned it was part of the ancient ritual where the bear _was_ the feast. Live and learn. This story is for absent friends (never absent from the heart).

BALTIC TANGO

Symington stared at the bear. It was made of concrete and held up a sign that probably said you couldn't park there in front of the arrivals door of the Helsinki airport. He couldn't read it because it was in that strange language that seemed to have far too many vowels in it. All the words in Finnish seemed too long.

He wished he were back in England.

There was a whole row of bears, he saw now. Symington had a sudden jolt of childish glee at the thought of them trotting along in a parade, off to the woods for their picnic. Do Finnish bears picnic in the woods?

He retrieved the crumpled bit of paper on which he'd printed her email. Bad enough he had to get instructions that way. Computers were a necessary evil, but he refused to give in to the omnipresent mobile phone neck bend even here in the land of Nokia. He carried the phone but he only used it, grudgingly, when it couldn't be avoided.

She had sighed at him. 'Can't you just put the details on your phone? You might lose that bit of paper.'

'I might lose the phone, too.' That was his state of mind lately. Everything was expendable. Except her: the woman. Or should that be The Woman, like Conan Doyle. Symington had devoured the books as a boy. That was back when he thought he would be one of the good guys. Sherlock Holmes referred to the only character to ever outwit him in that way. Symington could understand. His woman outwitted everyone. And it pleased him to have a secret name for her, something only he knew. Names were problematic anyway, he thought, as he looked around for the bus stop.

He had first known her as Deborah. She was a target. He was sent to Bruxelles to kill her. His first failed job. The boss wanted her dead and instead he had killed the boss and had gone off with Deborah and her notions. It was a fake name,

of course. She was fake in a lot of ways. She claimed to be
born in Wales and raised in Croydon, but as she relaxed
more around him he heard the Irish lilt that burnished her
words like the sun on Galway Bay.

She finally admitted that she came from Connemara,
but refused to tell him her given name. 'It's real old country
blather. One of those ugly old names my gran's best mate
had. Names that require phlegm and a good lungful of air
to pronounce.' Then she cleverly distracted him by undress-
ing to straddle him and he never asked again.

The thought of being inside her made his body ache.
It had only been three days since he'd been with her back
in Belgium but the sudden absence had left him dangling,
bereft. And horny. He'd been wanking like a teenager
in those three days, imagining himself burying his face
between her soft tits or spreading her thighs and hearing her
gasp. His cock stirred even now.

Fuck the bus. He hailed a cab, hoping the driver at least
spoke English. She had written down some helpful phrases
phonetically but he hadn't bothered to learn them. He didn't
have a head for things like that. Months in Belgium had not
got him much beyond 'merci' and 'au revoir' at best. He
wished he could go back to England.

'Can you take me here?' Symington thrust the folded
sheet of paper toward the driver, who glanced at the address
and gave a quick nod. They swung out the airport as he
stared at the bears. He'd be glad to see them again because it
would mean the job was done and they were heading home.

Not *home* home. He wasn't sure he had a home anymore.
At least not a place. The only place he felt at home was lying
with her, skin to skin. All the noise stopped and he didn't
have to think. A hotel room was enough for him. As long
as they had money to live on, he wouldn't bother stirring
further from her little flat than the restaurant that made the
great chips or that pub around the corner in Bruxelles. He
had to admit that he'd never seen himself as settling down
type, but maybe it was a kind of settling down.

Actually it wasn't so much settling as waiting to see what
happened next. With her, you never knew. That was part of
the excitement.

'You are English?' The cabbie looked up into the rearview mirror, a smile beaming. 'I recognize your accent. My cousin lives in London.'

'Ah,' Symington fumbled for something appropriate to say. He thought the man sounded Russian but maybe that was just how Finns sounded. He had no idea. There was a Finnish race car driver he sort of remembered—and wasn't the Celtic goalie Finnish, too? Not that he'd ever heard them talk. 'What does your cousin do?'

The cabbie laughed. 'He's a gangster. Aren't most Russians in London gangsters?'

Symington had no idea how to answer that. 'So, you're Russian?'

The man cocked an eyebrow at him. 'You didn't think I was a Finn did you?'

'I hardly know. I've never been to Finland before. What are they like?'

The cabbie seemed to mull this over. 'There are two kinds. There are winter Finns and summer Finns. Winter ones never say three words altogether. They tend to stare at their own shoes most of the time.'

'And summer Finns?'

'Oh they're quite outgoing. They stare at your shoes!' He laughed long and hard, actually wiping a tear away. 'They are very sporty. No matter the time of year. Skiing and running and swimming and always the sauna.'

'Sounds…energetic.'

'But they are funny. Very quietly so, but very funny. They like the absurd. Like you English. You like the absurd, yes?'

'I couldn't really say.'

The city streets surrounded them now after the rural landscapes near the airport. Maybe it was the effect of the cabbie's comments but he seemed to see sports arenas and sporting shops everywhere he looked. They crossed over tram lines and followed them along a main road, passing a venerable building with a massive bear outside it.

'What's with all the bears? I thought bears were a Russian thing.' The streets were crowded with folks, most of whom seemed preternaturally blonde and fit. It made him feel pudgy and very English.

'Oh, bears are ancient. Finns are all magic. Even the Vikings were afraid of them. You will hear the Bear Feast

Polska while you are here. Without a doubt. It is famous and old.'

Symington had no idea what that meant. The cab stopped. 'Here you are. Just down there. I can't pull up at the hotel itself, it is a pedestrian zone, but you can see the entrance, there.'

He paid the cabbie and saluted him as he pulled away into traffic. He walked up the narrow walkway between the buildings. Most of the signs in the cafés had English on them, which made him more hopeful. The people sitting at the tables and calling to each other on the street all looked blonde and young and happy. It was disconcerting.

He fumbled for the crumpled paper again as he needed the door code for the hotel. It seemed strange to have no concierge to meet him. Scandinavian efficiency, he supposed. Or was it Baltic? Finland was weirdly poised on a borderland between the two regions with Russia looming over it. It looked kind of Scandinavian but it didn't sound like it. All that mattered though is the number worked. He got in the tiny elevator and went up to his room and punched the buttons on the door.

The room was odd. There was a huge reproduction of some old painting all along the wall over the bed. The men were in strange old clothes and the women were naked. It seemed vaguely familiar. In the middle of the oblong room was a rosy red plastic bathroom unit that looked as if it had been dropped into the room by a crane. The toilet and shower were compact but you had to step up from the wood floor into the plastic unit. A table and chairs of matching red plastic filled up the space before the window. He twitched the curtain open.

Down below a restaurant sat empty. Round tables ready for patrons sat under an open gazebo frame. It looked like it should be outdoors but it was all inside. And completely empty. Symington shook his head. Just weird.

He texted her and didn't have to wait too long. Maybe she was in the same hotel. A furtive knock came at the door. He opened it and did a double take. 'You're blonde.'

'How do you like it?'

He closed the door behind her and started peeling off her clothes. She let him. He couldn't stop kissing her even as his hands worked at the buttons. His hands itched to be on her skin. 'You didn't dye that,' he said grabbing the hair on her mound and pulling her toward him.

'You know me. I'm lazy.' She let him throw her on the bed as he quickly shed his own clothes. He was so hard it ached. Nonetheless he paused long enough to drink in her curves with his eyes. God, she was lush. He felt the familiar urge to bite her soft flesh as he climbed on top of her.

'No marks,' she whispered, bringing his mouth back up to her own. 'Just in case.'

'In case what?' He was suspicious now, but his body over-ruled any coherent thought. He thrust inside her and they both groaned with satisfaction. He loved the sounds she made. And the way she moved under him threatened to make him come too fast so he stopped her moving, holding her arms down firmly. 'In case of what?'

She looked up at him with the smile he knew so well. It tipped into arrogance because she always figured she was the smartest one in the room. The Woman. Someday it might not be true, though it was just as likely she would adjust to that fact quickly and come up with something new. Her brain worked so quickly. 'They like saunas here. People get naked in them. I don't want to look too decadent. I'm supposed to be an executive.'

He laughed. 'Executives aren't decadent?'

'Men are funny about women in business. They want to think we're angels that they might get the chance to fuck. But one that no one else has fucked. They want to get in on the ground floor.'

Symington entwined his fingers with hers and raised their hands above her head. 'How is your ground floor?' He thrust into her with force. Her face contorted, eyes closed as she gasped. Her legs wrapped around his hips. 'It seems like an eternity since I was inside you.'

'Three days.'

'An eternity.' He couldn't wait any longer. He pounded against her, unconcerned whether it hurt her because some-times that was better and the fear that he needed her a lot more than she needed him always kept its cold hand on his neck and too soon he came, roaring like a bear. He collapsed on her, his head dizzy. His mouth went to her breast and he sucked hard while her fingers ruffled through his hair.

He rolled off her and looked at her face. The pale blue eyes looked right for the blonde hair but it was still strange to see her transformed again. Symington slipped his hand between her thighs, worried she had not been properly satisfied. He thrust his fingers inside her. So hot and so wet, it made him hungry again. In no time she was moaning and wriggling and he did not stop until he was sure he'd made her happy several times.

Almost at once he fell asleep, but she joggled him awake. 'We have to talk about the job.'

'Mmmhmmm,' he said, his fingers circling her thigh again.

'You are my colleague. You have to be doubtful about the business. Let him persuade you.'

'Right.' Her skin was like velvet. He leaned over to suck on her breast, tonguing her erect nipple with absurd happiness.

'Are you even listening?' She wrenched his head up with a fistful of hair. His mouth made a popping sound as it let go of her breast.

He gave her a great silly grin. 'Yes. What's his name again?'

'Matti Outinen.' She pronounced it precisely, with practiced ease. 'We're meeting him for dinner. Be nice, professional—you do have a better suit, right? One that doesn't make you look like a criminal?'

'Business drone blue, just like you said.' He tried to kiss her, but she was back in work mode, the brain ticking along like that precision timer. Giving up, he rolled onto his back, hands behind his head. His cock stirred a little, wanting more, not yet ready for it. He longed to bury himself in her again, always.

'If we can pull this off, we'll get a boatload of cash and we should go somewhere exotic and warm.' She sat up and swung her legs over the side. 'You ever been to Tangier?'

'No.'

'I think it would be nice.' She padded off to the cubicle to shower. There wasn't room enough for two and anyway, if she wanted him to join her he'd know. Symington inhaled. The room smelled like her now and that made him happy.

They were to meet up at 6 and head to the restaurant. Outinen would meet them there. It was some swanky joint down on the water's edge. You had to take a boat to get there. 'It's only open in the summer time,' she told him as she reapplied her makeup. 'He wants to make a good impression. Eager.'

'What does he do?'

She paused. 'He has a factory or factories, I suppose. He makes rubber ducks.'

'Like for the bath?' He laughed.

She grinned. 'Somebody has to do it. Other things too, but it's the ducks I remember.'

He lay back on the bed, considering the weirdness of that truth. Not that it mattered. He wasn't there to understand. Symington had no illusions about that. He didn't need to know the details of the gig. He was bones and muscle holding a club.

Watching her making up made him desire her again, but he knew it would be out of the question. Maybe a wank in the shower thinking about her, counting down the hours until she was back in his bed.

As long as she wasn't planning to be elsewhere. The knife in his gut was always ready to turn.

'Six sharp, in your blue suit, right?' She looked down at him as he fondled his cock staring into her eyes. 'Don't wear that out. I want you to make me scream later.'

'I'll get my belt out.' She left without even a kiss, afraid to muss her lipstick. Symington felt let down and a little anxious, as he always did when she left the room, fearing he would never see her, be inside her again. With her he was punching above his weight class and knew it. His only hope was to stay useful—indispensable even—and be ready to fuck her whenever and however she wanted.

He had absolutely no problem with that.

I clean up well enough, he decided as he checked his tie in the mirror where she had applied her makeup just a few hours before. He looked business-like, bland and unremarkable. A face in the crowd, never memorable: It suited the work. Symington moved to the window and stared down at the empty tables, shaking his head.

Her knock came on the hour like clockwork. The woman smelled of coffee and perfumes as if she had been lunching with suburban ladies. He didn't ask where she had been. It didn't matter, not much anyway. They took a cab to the harbor. The city came to him in glimpses out the window. Old buildings and new, a pretty park, some statues. Lots of people out strolling in the light. He'd forgotten how far north they were. Did the sun go down at all this time of year?

At the harbor the mark was there to meet them. He was tall, athletic looking, big shoulders, blonde of course with a ruddy face of good health, presumably from those outdoor games. He was a veritable bear of a man. 'Mr. Outinen, so good to see you. My colleague, Edward Sanders.'

Outinen grabbed his hand with relish and shook it vigorously, not in any stronger-than-thou aggressiveness but with a genuine sense of eagerness. 'Ms. Clair, Mr. Sanders! Let us be friends. I am Matti. Yes?'

'Call me Suzanne,' she said, dazzling him with a smile. It set off a song in Symington's head. The names had come from one of her favorite books, again. It was hard to keep up with them. 'And Ed, you don't mind do you?'

'Friendly is good.' He smiled. It was a faint echo of her sunshine, but he had no idea what his job would be this time. Maybe he wouldn't have to kill this man. He seemed nice enough.

Outinen steered the woman toward the dock where a boat awaited, his hand on her arm. 'This is the only way to get out to the restaurant, though it's only on the other end of this peninsula.' He spoke English with practiced ease though with the vowels longer as if he wanted to squeeze in all the extra Finnish ones somewhere.

They got onboard and in no time the little boat chugged out into the docks surrounded by loads of other little boats and some fancy sailboats or clippers or whatever they were called. Everybody who could afford it seemed to have one. It must be the status symbol of the city. They arrived at the destination quickly and got out. The open sea stretched before them and it made Symington feel a bit queasy.

'I reserved a table outside. Look! You can see the islands and just about see to Tallinn.' He squinted off into the sunlight. Sails dotted the gulf. 'There are the booze cruises to Estonia. You English invented that idea, I think.' Outinen laughed with hearty good humor. 'We have perfected it. Alcohol is so expensive here.'

They sat down and a waitress of very formal beauty appeared at once, greeting Outinen by name. He exchanged a few words with her, she handed out menus and then slipped away. 'I have order the starters for us. I insist! There is a treat you must share. The 'secrets of the island' it is called and very fine bites. And prosecco to wash it down. We must celebrate, my friends.'

'Indeed,' she purred back at him with a big smile over the menu. 'Everything looks so good, I can hardly choose.'

'Allow me to suggest,' Outinen said with sudden seriousness, going over the dinner items with her in detail. Symington knew the trick well. She pretended to be so helpless to play up to the big strong man. The Finn was eating out of her hand already. He hoped the job didn't include killing. This man would doubtless put up a good fight. It was easy to picture Outinen in one of those absurd Olympic contests, swimming, running, shooting—hell, the Finns probably invented some of them. His hands were massive. She laid her small hand on his arm and gave it a squeeze as she looked up into his eyes with a smile.

He would take his jealousy out on her later.

The waiter and the hostess brought the plate of starters and the ice bucket of prosecco. It was going to be a stylish meal. Symington sat up a little more stiffly, overcompensating for his discomfort in being out of his class. It was a lot easier to kill people than to dine formally with them. You could get a curry after and relax.

Eventually he did loosen up, about the time the second bottle of wine upturned its last. Outinen was immensely friendly and put them both at ease. He could tell she relaxed a bit too. The tight core of tension in her from always being on top of things didn't quite uncoil, yet it hummed a bit slower than usual. She drank more too, something she normally avoided. Maybe it was part of the plan.

Outinen advised them on all the things they must see in

Helsinki, from the statute of Havis Amanda where the students gathered on May Day to drink and throw their hats in the air to celebrate, to the home of the painter who painted the ancient stories, and museums of every kind. 'There is modern art too, if you like that sort of thing, Kiasma. I don't understand most of it. I like the historical museum.'

'That's the one with the bear?' She smiled and sipped her wine, washing down the last of her salmon which had been declared 'exquisite' at the first bite.

'What's with the bears?' Symington asked, surprising even himself. 'I saw them at the airport, too. Bears everywhere.' He was getting a bit tight, he could hear it in his voice. He set down the wine glass and went back to worrying the braised lamb.

Outinen grinned. 'The mead-paw, the honey-eater. The bear is our ancient symbol. He was here before the people and the memory of the world's founding is in him.' He said the words as if he believed them.

'And there's a bear feast?' The Woman was looking at him, brows furrowed. He ought to shut up. But what harm could come of it? The hook of curiosity and the devil-may-care spirit of the wine egged him on.

Outinen clapped his hands with delight. He fished in his pocket for his mobile. 'Listen!' He played a ringtone. '*Karhunpeijaispolska*. The Bear Feast Polska. You know it?'

'No, a cabbie mentioned it. I still don't understand.'

'Like the Teddy Bear's Picnic?' She said and he realized that she wasn't worried about the job, just annoyed at being out of the conversation. It wasn't the natural order of things.

'No, not that kind of feast.' Outinen frowned. 'The bear is the feast, you see.' He nodded.

Symington started. 'You eat bears?'

'We eat reindeer, too. Don't tell the children! Or Santa!' He laughed. 'In ancient days the bear was knowledge as well as food. The polska is his honor. The feast would respect the gift of the bear. They would mount his head and skin at the head of the table and people would raise a glass to him. Kippis!' Outinen knocked back another glass. None of the many glasses seemed to have the least effect on him. He'd heard that Finns had hollow legs.

'That's awful,' she said, clearly appalled by the image of the dead bear at the table.

'One cannot go through life without causing harm,' Outinen said with a shrug. 'It is best to honor those who fall.' He patted her arm as if to offer some comfort. Symington did his best to conceal the rage it sparked inside him.

Over pine tar ice cream and berry liqueurs, Outinen invited them out to his cottage outside the city. It sat on a small lake and naturally, had a sauna. 'To celebrate! All will be agreed to and yes, all will be happy. You must have a real sauna, not some hotel sauna. A real Finnish experience. Karhu beer and vodka.' He elbowed Symington in laddish solidarity. Outinen was all summer Finn. His car dropped them off near the hotel and they made their tipsy way inside.

He could tell she was not entirely pleased about something. However she did not object to stripping down and bending over as he doubled his belt and struck her repeatedly, reddening her cheeks and making her scream with pleasure until he could not wait any longer and buried himself in her from behind. The heat of his blows warmed her cheeks and despite the drunkenness he came fairly quickly, shuddering against her, his hands clutching the soft ripeness of her breasts as he cried out.

'Did you come?' he asked when his breathing slowed enough to make sentences. He untangled his limbs from hers and flopped down beside her on the bed.

'Yes, yes. Do you think he's on to something?' Her thoughts were not even in the room. After all he'd done for her. She loved the smack of his belt, the pain it caused, the welts it left. As if it absolved her of all wrong-doing. But it hurt him.

'Will you ever tell me the truth about anything?' He didn't mean to snap. It was more exasperation than anything else. Her distant expression and dismissive words annoyed him.

The question didn't anger her like he expected it to do. Instead she laughed. 'The truth? It should be used only sparingly.'

And like that his anger waned. 'Saved for special occasions, like?'

'Like your gran's best china.'

She didn't add that it was also because it was valuable, often ugly, inclined to be brittle and easily broken. He added that in his head while he stroked the welts on her backside with tenderness. 'We're bad people.' He kissed the red flesh.

The words hung in the air for a time between them. Then she sighed. 'We're not bad people. Just a bit reckless, that's all.'

The next day they followed Outinen in her rental car to the city's edge and into the countryside that rolled along beyond it: hills, lakes, white birch trees and here and there little red cottages. They didn't stop anywhere until they reached the turn off. Down a winding lane until they reached another little red cottage made of wood and beyond it the sparkle of a lake. It was like being in a fairy tale.

'Choose your bed!' Outinen told them as he carried in bags of food. 'I will get the fire going.'

Symington was nonplussed for a moment—a fire in this heat?—then he remembered the sauna. While it warmed he and Outinen drank beer with the grim bear face on it. KARHU it said in big letters. That was bear. So he knew one Finnish word.

She opted for a glass of wine instead and demurred on joining them in the sauna. 'I want to walk along the water. I miss being by the shore,' she said, tantalizing him with more elusive hints of her past. Connemara on the coast: he could picture her there as a teen in an Arran jumper, coppery hair blowing as she gazed out to sea. He watched her wander out the door, glass in hand, a mystery ever.

Outinen grabbed another four beers and set them down on the wooden table. 'We'll need these when we come out. For hydration. And then the sausages!' He stripped and Symington reluctantly did so too, absurdly conscious of his corpse-white skin. The sauna was a separate building from the cottage, made of honey-colored wood and sporting a shower on the outside. Outinen washed himself and then handed the soap to Symington to do the same. The bar smelled like pine trees. They stepped inside to a kind of antechamber which was already surprisingly hot.

'This is the *vihta*,' Outinen said handing him a bundle of leaves and twigs. 'Gets the circulation going.' Then they stepped inside and the full heat of the sauna blasted into his face.

'At least it's a dry heat,' Outinen said, slapping him on the shoulder as he climbed to the top bench. Symington sat nearby but not quite as high, figuring the heat might be a little less. He'd been in steam rooms before. Dry or not, this seemed to be a whole lot hotter. Sweat emptied from every pore. He wondered how long he could take it.

For a time they both remained silent, then Outinen spoke softly, 'Women used to give birth in the sauna. It is the most hygienic place. It keeps us healthy and strong.' He laughed and began to smack himself with the branches.

Symington followed suit. It felt strange, but it was better than just sitting there. The leaves filled the wooden room with an earthy fragrance. He supposed it would promote the ruddy good health enjoyed by Outinen and all the Finns he saw on the streets, but he couldn't wait until this bizarre ritual was over.

'We have many sauna traditions,' Outinen said as he set down the leafy flogger. 'There is the sauna elf or fairy, I suppose you would say—the *saunatonttu*. Warring clans would hold their negotiations in the sauna because only soft words should be spoken here.' He laughed. 'So I brought you here.'

Symington stiffened. 'Oh?'

'Are you completely on board with this project?'

He relaxed a bit. 'I trust my colleague.' For the life of him, he couldn't remember her fake name. Suzanne, that was it. Suzanne who takes you down. 'Suzanne is pretty sharp.'

'How deeply are you in with her?' The voice was gentle, a father getting to the bottom of things, sorting out a childish spat.

'How deeply?'

Outinen clicked his tongue. 'Don't play dumb.'

'I'm not playing,' Symington said with a shrug. 'I don't know what you're asking.'

'I know these deals are risky always. But I've looked into things and she doesn't check out. You, I don't have enough data yet. You might be all right. But you should be frank with me.'

Despite the heat a chill shot up his spine. He wished for a gun, not to mention a hat and a coat. His pudgy flesh made him vulnerable. Stuck in a vacation home in the country with nothing for life insurance. He needed a drink. 'I think I'm ready for that beer.'

'We need to talk,' Outinen said, but Symington rose and headed for the door. He could feel his heartbeat accelerate, as much from moving in the unaccustomed heat as from the sudden surge of adrenaline.

'I should hate to have to bring the authorities into things,' Outinen said with an air of regret. 'My behavior won't look good. But we can still sort things out.'

'I need a drink first.'

'A better cut for me will be necessary of course,' Outinen said. The coldness in his voice left no doubt about how big that cut was going to be.

It had all gone south so fast.

Symington stepped into the sunlight blinking. *Get the phone.* He can't call anyone then. Did he have a gun somewhere? Probably not. But you never know. He might keep a skeet shooting rifle on the mantel or some other sporty thing. Fortunately Outinen had left his phone on top of the neatly folded clothing he'd shed so it was easy to grab.

He dressed hastily, shoving the phone into his trouser pocket. Where had she gone? He would have to find her and they could finagle an escape back to the city before he could alert others. Maybe they could subdue him, tie him up until they were on their way. They could get away by boat if they couldn't get a flight.

Symington continued buttoning his shirt as he broke into a ragged gait. His head was light, probably dehydrated. He should have drunk a beer. Where was she? Just like her to disappear when he could use her quick thinking.

He could hear Outinen behind him and moved his feet a little faster. He glanced over his shoulder. The man had not wasted time dressing. Symington stopped at the water's edge, glancing left and right. He couldn't see her anywhere.

Out on the bay a small sailboat moved across the water but there was no one else to be seen.

Outinen's feet pounded on the soft ground as he ran toward the water. Symington wasn't sure what would happen when he got there and he had no idea how he ought to behave. The man was hollering at him. His head filled with a blind panic. As the naked man came up, he grabbed Symington by the shoulders and instinct took over. Adrenaline made his limbs react.

They grappled on the water's edge. Symington's foot slipped into the water with a splash as he did his best to shove Outinen back. The pleasant face wore an expression of concentration without malice. It struck him that they must look comical fighting like this. Him shambolically dressed and the Finn naked like a Greek wrestler.

It was hard to take it seriously even as he shoved back against the man's grip. He hadn't fought hand-to-hand since he was a boy. His job consisted of lying in wait in the right place to dispatch people with a gun and a silencer. The problem with wrestling like this was he was too damn old and way out of shape. The only exercise he got anymore was in bed with her.

Where was she?

Symington stepped back and at once sensed his error. First he battled to right his balance but it was too late, and though it seemed to take an eternity they both fell, Outinen on top of him. They grunted as their bodies landed, scrambling with splashes and thuds. Water got in his ears and increased the sense of panic. He shoved the man off him.

Symington wriggled up out of the water, spitting and coughing, trying to shake the water out of his ears. Outinen got up too but looked dazed. His forehead was bleeding. He must have hit it on one of the rocks that had tripped up his own feet. He reached for Outinen's neck, but missed his grasp on the slick wet flesh while the other man grabbed the fabric of his trousers and drew him back down.

With fear fueling a growing sense of desperation, Symington brought his knee up to the man's groin. The look on Outinen's face was a priceless mixture of surprise and disappointment, as if he could not believe a man would sink so low.

Desperate times called for desperate measures: Symington had no intention of playing the gentleman.

Outinen fell into the water, sputtering and groaning. Symington looked up to see her, frozen at the water's edge. Her eyes were wide. 'Help me,' he hissed. His opponent was struggling up. She didn't move although her eyes followed them both.

Symington heaved himself on top of Outinen. With an effort he brought his elbow up to the man's neck and leaned his weight on it. The Finn struggled in earnest now. He could use her help but she made no move to lend a hand. The two men's bodies entwined in an absurd parody of coupling that threatened to make him laugh if it weren't for the effort of holding the man's face down in the water.

After a time the bubbles stopped. The only breath he heard was his own.

'Is he dead?'

He looked up at her. She didn't look frightened or alarmed really. He was having a hard time figuring out what she was thinking. But she was thinking. 'Yes.'

'Fuck.'

Symington staggered to his feet. The body jiggled with the tide but did not otherwise move. 'We're fucked. He was going to turn us in. His people found information on you.'

Her mouth formed a hard line. 'Let's get out of here.'

'Give me the glass.' He took it from her hand and dashed it on the biggest rock he could see. There was something satisfying in the sound of breaking glass. Let them think Outinen had stumbled and drunkenly drowned.

They cleared out the cottage. She frowned at him when he threw several beers into his gym bag, but said nothing. He needed a drink or several. They'd have to make a quick exit from the hotel, too. She would have to talk fast at the airport to get their flight changed and it would cost them.

Not as much as it had cost Outinen.

In the strange little hotel room he changed into dry clothes and emptied three beers while he waited for her. It crossed his mind a few times that she might not return, yet he felt only the dull ache of it. She was back before the beer buzz began to hit him.

He opened the door to her soft knock and she stepped in quickly as if afraid of being seen. 'You want the last beer?'

'You've had all of them?'

'Not this one.' She shook her head so he opened it and drank down the bear's golden nectar.

'You're going to spend the entire flight pissing,' she said, though it wasn't as if she hadn't seen him drink plenty before.

'Why didn't you help me?' he asked, his voice barely above a whisper because he wasn't sure he wanted to ask it.

Maybe she hadn't heard him. But after a moment she said, 'I never killed anyone.'

Symington belched. 'Are you sure?'

Her look said he'd be paying for that question for a very long time, but he didn't take it back.

As they pulled up at the airport, he saw the bears all in a row. He couldn't help thinking 'karhu' and promised himself he would drink to Outinen's memory. He wasn't a bad guy. Seemed a shame to kill someone so healthy and friendly. But there were all kinds of reasons people had to die.

He sat in the bar while she turned in the car key and sorted the tickets. There would be no Algiers now. No, wait—it was Tangier, wasn't it? 'Give me a Karhu,' he told the bartender. 'Kippis,' he said as he raised the glass, wishing he had the can instead. 'To absent friends.'

She came up and sat on the stool next to him, shaking her head at the bartender. 'Back to Belgium for now,' she said with a shrug.

With her blonde hair she could pass for a local. He wondered what she was thinking. Maybe he should wonder that more often if he didn't want to end up as dead as Outinen. She looked fine sitting there, but for the first time Symington wasn't counting the minutes until he could have her skin next to his. She gave him a wan smile.

'Penny for your thoughts?'

He didn't know what to say. 'I was thinking about the bear feast. What do you suppose it tastes like?'

She stared at him and then laughed. 'You're so…odd.'

'Didn't you wonder?'

'No, I can't say that I did.' They asked the bartender,

who shrugged and pretended not to understand the question. 'Probably tastes like chicken,' she finally said, looking at him with something like affection. 'Isn't that what they always say?'

Maybe everything would be all right, he told himself. She touched up her lipstick while he drank the rest of the bear beer. They had a plane to catch.

This tale is for Mary & Papa Bear: the tonttu is a house spirit who protects your home. You would be wise to treat your tonttu with kindness and generosity.

CONFABULATION

'It's what?' Eeva shook her head as if her ears had not heard right because there was something in them.

'We call the condition 'confabulation'—it's not voluntary.' The nurse practitioner smiled for a moment. Eeva had the impression that was all the time she had to smile that day because it lasted little more than a second.

'Confabulation,' she repeated, no closer to understanding. Her mother Hetti looked away, out the window that faced the street below as if completely unconcerned with their conversation. 'I don't think I know what you're saying.'

'It's a memory disturbance. Patients fabricate or distort their recollection of events.'

Eeva flushed. 'You mean she's lying.'

'I'm not lying,' her mother said at once. Her expression looked not so much annoyed as incredulous.

'She's not lying.' The nurse practitioner shook her head. 'Not deliberately. She believes completely the truth of what she's saying.'

'But what she's saying is mad,' Eeva said, shaking her head slowly.

'I'm right here, you don't have to talk about me as if I weren't.' Her mother glared at the two of them. 'And I'm not five years old. I can speak for myself. Besides, she told you I'm not crazy, so you should believe her.'

'She said you weren't lying, she didn't say you weren't crazy.' Eeva laid a hand on her mother's arm to soften the words. It was all so confusing. Her mother had always been the lynch pin of the family, the one who kept things together while her somewhat dreamy father had often been away in his own world—his books, his forest, his thoughts. Eeva had taken for granted the fact that her mother would always be managing things, while she had spent her whole life waiting for her father to pay some attention to anything she did, but he never really did. 'That's nice,' he'd say whether she showed him a drawing she made at five or the degree she received at thirty. And then he would talk about whatever was occupying his thoughts at that moment—some obscure folk song and how it made its way across Europe or a very interesting book he'd been reading about plumbing in ancient Rome. It didn't matter: it was always more interesting than what she was doing—unless he had a story to tell. He always had time to tell the old stories. Eeva grew up with a rich appreciation for the folktales of the old country.

He died two years ago, killed in the woods on their farm by a dead tree he'd gone to cut down. Hetti had gone out to find him, taken care of all the necessities for his burial and held everyone together while they mourned. She did it with the same dogged patience with which she approached washing the windows or chopping kindling. Perhaps it was to be expected that at last she would have to suffer some fallout from the grief. But she had got so weak so fast.

'You have to be sensible,' Eeva told her, as if she could scold her mother out of this state of—what was it? Confabulation. Honestly, it sounded like an invented disease. She wondered for the umpteenth time whether doctors simply sat around creating new syndromes which they could then medicate and charge outrageous sums to treat. It seemed insane that health care still operated as a profit industry. 'I don't know why you're being so silly.'

'I might ask you the same thing,' Hetti said, folding her arms. Her annoyance radiated like fire's crackle. 'If you would just do as I said—'

Eeva laughed and looked to the practitioner for support, but she was looking at her watch instead.

Noticing the silence, the woman looked up and gave another quick smile. 'I have rounds to complete. As long as your mother poses no risk, she can stay.' The woman touched Hetti's arm lightly and twirled away to walk down the corridor with a brisk but silent step. Hospital shoes seemed to make no sound. It was a bit unnerving.

The words took a moment to sink in: ...*she can stay.* Eeva had not even contemplated the idea of having to move her mother somewhere else. A weight descended upon her with unexpected force. She turned back to her mother who was looking a bit bored now. 'Mama, you have to stop saying outrageous things.'

'It's not outrageous. You always believed in *tontut*. You used to feed our *kotihaltija* at night.'

'I was five years old. I'm a bit past the believing in elves and fairies stage, mother,' Eeva said although she felt a pang of guilt. 'I'm not going to believe that our house elf has come here to speak to you.'

'Of course not,' Hetti said. 'That would be ridiculous.'

'I'm glad you agree, mama.'

'It was the *tonttu* for this place.'

Eeva groaned. 'This place has a *tonttu*?'

'Every place has a t*onttu*,' her mother said. 'Everyone knows that.'

Eeva sighed and sat back down on the uncomfortable chair next to her mother's bed. 'But what's that got to do with anything? Mama, you have to stop sounding crazy. I can't really afford to move you to another place. You need some help with care. And you refused to stay at home with us.'

'You live in that itty bitty, cramped place, all three of you. It's madness.' Her mother shook her head, disbelieving.

'We're quite comfortable. Cozy. We like it.' The last thing Eeva wanted was to talk about their tiny flat. It was the best they could afford right now, what with Mikael working in the city and the non-stop business meetings he had to be there for. He was making a name, soon they'd be better off: they both knew the drill. Eeva could do her sketches and design anywhere, scan them in and email them off. It was fine. She had to admit that after growing up on the farm and in the forest at times it felt like a cage, but what could they do with the housing market as it was? 'It suits us.'

'You could take over the farm.' Hetti's face pinched with pain.

'Mama, it's still your home.' Eeva took her mother's hand and squeezed it. Those were the last words she expected to hear today and it made her stomach clench. Up 'til now her mother had spoken of returning to the house 'when she mended' but now—well, the truth must have sunk in.

Hetti patted her daughter's hand. 'The *tonttu* scolded me for hanging on to what I could not use. Pass it along. He said there's a ritual to be done first, however.'

'And what's that?' Eeva smiled. If this was her mother's way of dealing with letting go of the farm, so be it. It was a lot better than her being crazy.

'You have to burn the tree that killed your father.'

'What?' Of all the things she might have guessed, she never expected that. Eeva thought her mother would want some small, token gesture—what? Lighting a candle or making a wish seemed the sort of thing. What did she know of ritual? The tree that killed him! There was something horrid about the idea of going back to that spot. Surely even her mother would resist such a thing. 'Mama, you can't mean that.'

'Go out there, chop it up, burn it and say goodbye to the past. We have to clear the way to the future.' Her mother sounded remarkably decisive.

'The *tonttu* told you that?' Eeva felt a ringing in her head as if a headache were coming on.

'Well, he got it from our *kotihaltija*—and don't ask me how.' She threw her hands up as if in defeat of a huge bureaucracy. 'Who knows how they pass along information? I don't know. Magic, I guess.'

Eeva stared at her mother and then burst into laughter. 'Yes, I suppose that must be it.'

Later as she drove home in the twilight, her tired old red Honda wheezing at the stop lights, Eeva wondered if insanity were not catching. Yes, there must be some sort of network for house elves. 'I want to make a *tonttu*-to-*tonttu* call. Yes, please reverse the charges.' She only knew the phrases from old movies. Everyone had worldwide phone calling ability at their fingertips.

Eeva shook her head. Forget the nonsense, focus on what must be done. But what should she do? She sighed. *I'll talk it over with Mikael.* When she had gone round and round in circles in her head, it always helped to talk to him and stop the merry-go-round in her brain. Eeva could count on him to go straight to the most obvious answer when she had run off on every tangent getting lost.

For once he was home when she got there, too. He was on the floor with Oskar building bizarre Lego contraptions on wheels that fell over as soon as you tried to roll them on the carpeting because they were far too tall and top-heavy. 'How's your mother?' her husband asked, rising to his feet and cursing only for a moment as he stepped on a stray block. He leaned over to kiss her after she threw herself down on the sofa. The warmth of his lips filled her with calm happiness.

'She's…all right. Just a bit odd. The staff doesn't think it's much to worry about. Probably,' she added with a frown. 'But she has a little task for us.'

'A task?' Mikael threw himself down on the sofa beside her and slung his arm around her shoulders. He was a big bear of a man, not much given to chatter, but when he spoke he always said something thoughtful. Eeva liked to think he had the best qualities of both her parents: a sharp mind, but a practical outlook, a bit quiet but not because he was distracted. Mikael was always paying attention. She learned that early on in their relationship. Accustomed to hiding her problems from other people, Eeva had been unprepared when he insisted not only on knowing why she was out of sorts but also on coming up with a reasonable approach to her problems.

It took some getting used to.

'What is that thing?' She leaned forward to take a closer look at Oskar's peculiar vehicle. The boy had quite an imagination.

'It's for people who work in tall buildings, so they don't have to take the stairs when they get to work.' The car immediately fell over, exposing a key design flaw, but Oskar did not seem to mind. 'Maybe I should give it wings.'

'They will help balance it.' He was her stepson but she'd been the only mother he had for most of his life. Eeva hadn't realized that Mikael had a son when she first started seeing him. And even when she figured it out, it didn't seem like that big of a deal. She was just grateful that he seemed to like her. Eeva had never had much experience with kids. Growing up her friends had all done babysitting for pocket money. Her allowance for doing chores was generous enough to cover the books and art supplies she wanted, so she had never been interested in pursuing extra work.

Without realizing how it happened, Eeva had come to love Oskar the way she loved Mikael. For a time she had held them both at arm's length not because she cared to little but rather because it never failed to surprise her that she cared so much. Her way had always been so solitary; her parents were happy to leave her to her own devices for long periods of time and she had mostly reveled in the freedom it offered her. Her drawing skills had been well developed long before she went off to art school. Eeva had enjoyed the startled looks of her instructors as they examined her work and then modified assignments to ask more of her. She had found work before completing her degree due to her assured skills and flexibility at coming up with a variety of ideas for any project. After all, it was how she had always amused herself.

In the last few years, however, Eeva had become a little terrified at the horrible fragility of things. Her father's death was a terrible blow, but somehow her mother's dwindling abilities struck harder. Eeva had never really been the first line of defense for anything. She had always had other people she could rely on.

'So,' Mikael said, breaking into her thoughts. 'Pizza night?'

'Yay, pizza night!' Oskar's vote was cast.

Eeva laughed. 'The usual order?' Clearly Mikael had figured out she wasn't ready to talk yet. She made the call and they enjoyed the usual boisterous pizza night chatter which distracted her for a good while. After they put Oskar to bed, playing one last video game on his handheld, Eeva felt a twinge of guilt. She should be teaching him the old stories as her father had done, not sending him to sleep with the jangling noise of some commercially produced game.

But she was no story teller; her skills were with images. Maybe a picture book before he got too old for it. Or comics? That was an interesting idea. She'd have to mull that over. It had potential as a commercial project, which was never a bad thing.

Her mind was turning over the comic book idea as they got into bed. So she was taken by surprise when Mikael asked about her mother. 'What?'

'I take it there was something you didn't want to talk about. Maybe because Oskar was there?'

Eeva sighed. 'Well, it's a bit strange. It wasn't anything medical, I mean not really. But they had a word for it, called it 'confabulation'.' She shrugged. 'It just seemed that she was making things up, but they said it was—oh, I don't know exactly.'

Mikael nodded as if he understood. It always meant that he was willing to listen further. He took his time jumping in. He liked to be sure she'd said all she had on her mind first, as if she would be startled away like a deer. 'What kind of things?'

She covered her face with her hands and groaned. 'Talking to a *tonttu*.'

'Hunh.'

Eeva looked at Mikael. 'You don't seem too surprised.'

'Well, I suppose it depends on what the *tonttu* is telling her.'

Eeva laughed. 'You're willing to believe she believes she's been talking to elves, though?'

'It seems harmless enough,' Mikael said. 'As long as it's not advising her to foment revolution or start fires. It's not is it?'

'No. Well, yes actually.'

Mikael's eyebrows shot up. 'Which one?'

'Fire. The *tonttu* said we need to burn the tree that killed my father.'

Mikael winced. 'Well, I suppose there's some poetic justice in that.'

'Ritual, that was the word she used. The *tonttu* said we'd have to chop up the tree and burn it to move on, I guess. For her to let go. That's the other thing. She said we should take the farm. I couldn't believe it.'

'Why not?'

Eeva stared at him, but Mikael was staring off into space or rather into the blue walls of the bedroom. She had been glad they painted the room over but sometimes the color seemed too bright for sleep. 'Why not? Well, we can't just… move there.'

'We should think about it.' He yawned. 'Do you have to be up early tomorrow?'

'Me? No. But you don't mean it, do you? How could we manage getting back and for the to the city, or rather you doing it. Especially when winter comes. Think how much more trouble snow would be.' Eeva shook her head. It was madness.

Mikael yawned again. 'So we could go out this weekend and burn the tree, I suppose.' He slipped down under the covers with a happy sigh. 'I am tired tonight. It's been a long week and it's only Tuesday.'

'You want to go out there this weekend? I thought we were going to try to get some shopping done. Oskar's growing out of clothes so fast.'

'We can do both.'

Eeva took a long time to fall asleep, long after Mikael was snoring peacefully. *Why not?* Could it really be so simple? No, it simply wasn't practical. Think of being out there in the woods in the winter time. But then think too of how wonderful it would be to tramp through the woods with Oskar and show him all the wonders around the place. They had sold off most of the farm lands when her father got too old to keep the place going even with help. Their neighbors grew the same crops so at least it looked the same as ever when Eeva was there. He wasn't that old, but the hard life of farming had taken its toll. He was ten years older than her mother—and her mother had been an unusual thirty-three when she was born. They had given up on the idea that they would have a child and then she arrived.

But the woods—her father would not countenance any talk of selling them. They snuggled around the back of the house like a protective army, cut through with the little stream that howled in the spring flood and dribbled to little more than a whisper in the height of summer. And how did the trees pay him back? By killing him. Eeva sighed. He should have asked for help, not stubbornly gone out there on his own. What had he been thinking? Probably about Cicero's last speech or some old folk magic tale, she knew. Anything but the task in front of him.

Maybe if they did this thing it would help. It would get her mother over this strange obsession with the *tonttu* and back to herself. They all would feel a lot better then. Eeva closed her eyes and cuddled up to Mikael's broad back. Maybe it would be all right. At least he didn't seem to mind.

Oskar was all excited about the trip and bounced up and

down in the car with excitement. 'Are we really going to burn the tree?'

'We have to chop it up first,' his father told him. 'We'll make a bonfire. But it will take some time to get that done.'

'A lot of carrying of wood,' Eeva added. 'Your arms will be twice the length they are now by the end of the day.'

'They will not!' Oskar laughed anyway. He did not see the task ahead as work, which was just as well. He ran into the house to touch all his favorite things the moment Eeva unlocked the door. The boy was fascinated by the old bearskin that still covered the bed in the guest room. Eeva could hear him growl at it.

Oskar poked his head in the kitchen where they were putting the food they'd brought into the old Frigidaire. Mikael shook his head in wonder every time they came, unable to believe it was still running. 'Are we staying here tonight? Can I sleep in the bear room?'

'Yes and yes,' his father said.

'Hurrah!' Oskar ran off to go jump on the bear.

'We should get rid of the dusty old thing,' Eeva said, wrinkling her nose at the thought of what all might be living in the fur.

'I love the old things here. Even that.' Mikael nodded at the woodstove her mother still insisted in cooking on.

'I'll take gas. I got tired of chopping kindling when I was ten.'

'We could always have it adapted to gas, I bet.'

Eeva looked up. 'You're seriously thinking about us moving out here?'

Mikael shrugged. 'Can't hurt to think about it.'

They headed out of the house together. The sun had decided to show its strength that day and gave a fair showing. Though it had been a wet spring the day felt warm with almost a hint of summer to it. Oskar ran for the woods, but Eeva called him back.

'We need to stop at the barn first. Saws, hatchets and wheelbarrows.'

'Do I get to use the chainsaw?'

'No!' Mikael and Eeva said together.

Loaded up with equipment, they trundled the wheelbarrows out into the woods. Eeva tried to point out as many landmarks as possible to Oskar, feeling as if she had neglected this part of his education so far. 'When we had horses, I'd use that rock to get up in the saddle when I was too small. And that big stump? My dad carved my kantele out of that tree when we cut it down.'

'The one you let me play? The little five string one?'

'Yup. My dad made that.' Eeva remembered sitting for hours on the stump, strumming away at the strings as she thought about nothing at all really, just enjoying the music as it echoed through the trees.

Up over the rise they came to the grove where the broken beech lay. Moss had grown on the side of it. Untouched for two years now, she couldn't say she was surprised, but it made Eeva feel a little stab of pain thinking of moss covering her father. He had refused to be buried, wanted his organs donated and his ashes scattered in the fields he had ploughed so long. The tree had meant his death, but it was also the only tangible connection to his death.

'Are you all right with this?' Mikael put an arm around her waist and gave her a little squeeze. 'We don't have to do it if you'd rather we didn't.'

'No, I'm okay with it. It needs to be done.'

'We don't want the *tonttu* to be unhappy,' Oskar said with grave seriousness.

Eeva looked up. 'You know about that, eh?'

Oskar nodded. 'Will I see the *tonttu*? I've never seen one before. They are real aren't they. It's not like Santa.' He had felt very grown-up when he explained to Mikael that he knew the jolly fat man was really them.

'I haven't seen one since I was little,' Eeva said. 'Maybe he will come out when he sees we are serious about work. They expect you to work hard.'

Work hard they did. Mikael fired up the chainsaw—it made Eeva too nervous to use it—and began to work through the thick trunk, while she used the big axe to chop off smaller branches. Oskar dragged the smaller branches over to the wheelbarrows and with both of them looking on nervously, very carefully chopped them into smaller pieces. They worked for a couple of hours without stopping more than a few minutes, then loaded up the wood they had and wheeled it over to the bonfire pit.

'We haven't had a fire since Papa died,' Eeva said with a start. It had been such a ritual for midsummer and midwinter. They had sat spent months piling up rubbish. scrub wood, cleared brush and cardboard for the big fire. The ring of stones still marked the space but it looked worn and neglected.

'That will make Granddad happy,' Oskar said. He usually remembered the idea of his grandfather more than the reality, but Eeva was always surprised how strong that idea remained. Perhaps because he adored his grandmother, too. Mikael's parents lived so far away, the boy had not had a chance to really bond with them and Eeva suspected proximity would not change that much. They weren't the most welcoming people her own experience suggested.

When they had built the first ragged shape of the pyre, it was time to stop for sandwiches. Before they had finished eating, Mikael nudged Eeva and she saw that Oskar was falling asleep in his plate. They carried him off to the bear room, protesting sleepily that he didn't need a nap.

'Should we take a nap, too?' Mikael asked, stretching his arms up over his head and nearly hitting the rack of pots and pans that hung from the ceiling of the kitchen.

'If I take a nap now, I will sleep the day away,' Eeva said, a hand to her back as she stretched. 'I'm not used to this kind of physical labor anymore.' They headed back out, pushing the wheel barrows before them and set to work doggedly chopping at the wood.

'It's not like we have to do all of it today,' Mikael said at one point, setting down the axe to mop his brow. 'We have done an awful lot. And if we are moving out here, we'll have plenty of time to get it all.'

Eeva had been lifting the axe for another blow but stopped to look closely at him. 'Are you really thinking we could do that? I mean, what if Mama changes her mind? I mean if she starts feeling better and wants to come home?'

'We could all live here. I think she'd enjoy it now.' Mikael sat down on the chunk of wood he had started to split.

Eeva leaned on the axe. She didn't quite know what to say. The thought of living here awoke so many different things in her heart. 'But surely…it's impractical, don't you think? With all your meetings and late nights and whatnot?'

Mikael shrugged. 'You know how Bert Jenkins is always trying to get me to take a teaching position in the business school.'

'Bert! But you always turned him down. I don't want you to think, I mean, to feel obligated—' Eeva felt guilty like she had tricked him into something. She hadn't meant to do so. Maybe she shouldn't have told him about the thing with her mother.

'I never took it because I knew that I wouldn't make as much money as I would in the firm. But you know, if we lived here,' Mikael opened his hands to the woods around them, 'we would live much better on less. Instead of rent on that tiny flat, we could be investing in improvements to the house and barn. And getting Wi-Fi so you could work.'

'What do you think Oskar would say?' Eeva's heart suddenly seemed to be beating faster.

Mikael laughed. 'He would love it, you know he would. All we'd have to say is that he gets the bear room.' They both laughed.

'Can it be that easy?' Eeva walked over to where Mikael sat and put her hands on his shoulders. 'Can we just change everything like that?'

'Why not?' Mikael covered her hands with his own larger hands. 'What could be easier. We just say yes.'

Eeva laughed. 'I think I am very lucky to have stumbled across you.'

'Yes, you are.' He looked up and she leaned down to kiss him and they didn't see Oskar come trotting up, still rubbing his eyes.

'You let me sleep,' he said accusingly as he took up his little hatchet.

'You needed the rest,' his father said, his voice serious.

'I saw the *tonttu*,' Oskar told him as he hacked halfway through a small branch and then struggled to get the hatchet free.

'Oh you did, did you?' Eeva chuckled. She went to pick up her axe as Mikael retrieved his.

'What did he look like?' Mikael asked.

Oskar considered the question carefully. 'He had a blue shirt and a red cap, one of those funny ones that goes up.'

He made the shape over his own head. 'He said if we live here we have to follow the rules.'

Eeva and Mikael exchanged a glance. 'Maybe he overheard us?' He shrugged.

'Are there a lot of rules?'

'I don't know, he didn't say. He seems kind of stern but not so bad.'

'Stern, that's a good word,' his father said with approval. 'I'm glad you know it.'

Oskar looked at him with narrowed eyes. 'You're making fun of me.'

'Not at all.'

'You don't believe I saw the *tonttu* but I did.'

'I believe you,' Eeva said. 'Did he say anything else?'

Oskar brightened. 'He said the bear wants to go to the fire tonight.'

'The bear? Does he want to be in the fire?'

Oskar looked horrified. 'No, he just wants to see it.'

Mikael nodded. 'Okay then.' He looked around for the splitting maul which had gotten under some of the wood.

'So are we moving here?' Oskar insisted.

Mikael looked over at Eeva and smiled. 'Yes, we are.'

'Can I have the bear room?'

'I told you.'

Eeva laughed. 'Yes, you get the bear room. But you may have to share it with the *tonttu*.'

'Oh, he lives in the woods. He told me.' Oskar set to work very earnestly on the wood, determined to add to the fire.

'What was that word again?' Mikael asked as they stacked the next round of logs on the wheel barrows.

'What word? Oh, confabulation?' Eeva looked at him. He had wood chips in his hair, but he still looked handsome—and very happy.

Mikael held up the axe as if it were a sword. 'Then I declare it. From this time forward let us remember this as Confabulation Day and every year, let us celebrate it with wood, fire and our *tonttu*.'

'And sandwiches,' Oskar added.

'Yes, and sandwiches.'

'You idiot,' Eeva said, laughing despite herself.

'We few, we happy few—'

'Grab that wheel barrow, my king. We've got a fire to build.'

'A horse, a horse, my kingdom for a horse!' Mikael shouted, brandishing the axe before he buried it in the stump. The set off across the uneven ground. Oskar pretended to be a horse as he ran beside the wheel barrows and they all laughed like a bunch of crazy people, but it felt just fine.

APPENDIX:

Intrigued by Finnish Folklore?

The stories in UNIKIRJA stories were inspired, first and foremost, by the mythic poems collected and compiled by Elias Lönnrot, published as *The Kalevala* and *The Kanteletar*. These titles can be found in a variety of English translations, but I recommend these two in particular:

The Kalevala: Epic of the Finnish People. [By Elias Lönnrot.] Translated by Eino Friberg. Editing and Introduction by George C. Schoolfield. Illustrated by Björk Landström. Otava Publishing Company, 1988. ISBN-10: 9511101374; ISBN-13: 978-9511101376.

The Kanteletar: Lyrics and Ballads after the Oral Tradition. By Elias Lönnrot. Translated by Keith Bosley. Oxford University Press, 1992. ISBN-13: 978-0192828620.

I mention the following books as well in the introductions to the UNIKIRJA stories. They provided me with background information and inspiration.

Carter, Angela. *The Bloody Chamber*. Penguin, 1990. ISBN-10: 014017821X; ISBN-13: 978-0140178210.

Gaup, Ailo. *The Shamanic Zone*. Translated by Lasse V. Gundersen. Three Bears Company, 2005. ISBN-10: 8299696828.

Gender and Folklore: Perspectives on Finnish and Karelian Culture. Edited by Satu Apo, Aili Nenola, and Laura Stark-Arola. [Studia Fennica: Folkloristica 4.] Finnish Literature Society, 1998. ISSN 1235-1946; ISBN 9517178360.

Koppana, K. M. *Snake Fat and Knotted Threads: An Introduction to Traditional Finnish Healing Magic.* Heart of Albion Books, 2003. ISBN-10: 1872883656; ISBN-13: 978-1872883656.

Sell, Anja. *Laulupiiri: Saestykset / Singing Circle: Accompaniments.* 2000. Published by the author: 725 Copeland Street, Madison WI, 53711.

Stark, Laura. *The Magical Self: Body, Society and the Supernatural in Early Modern Rural Finland.* [Folklore Fellows' Communications, vol. CXXXVIII, no. 290.] Suomalainen Tiedeakatemia, 2006. ISSN 0014-5815; ISBN-10: 9514109988.

Stark-Arola, Laura. *Magic, Body and Social Order: The Construction of Gender Through Women's Private Rituals in Traditional Finland.* [Studia Fennica: Folkloristica 5.] Finnish Literature Society, 1998. ISSN 1235-1946; ISBN-10: 9517460511.

COPYRIGHT
ACKNOWLEDGEMENTS

'Darkest Day' first published as 'Sun Thief' in 'Swords and Sorceress XXI' DAW Books. Copyright © 2004 K.A. Laity

'Kerttu' first published by 'New World Finn' 2004. Copyright © 2004 K.A. Laity

'Palakainen' first published in 'New World Finn' 2007. Copyright © 2007 K.A. Laity

'Sinikka Journeys North' first published in 'The Beltane Papers' 2001, reprinted in 'Mythic Passages' 2004. Copyright © 2004 K.A. Laity

'Vipunen' first published in New World Finn 2005, reprinted in 'Mythic Passages' 2007. Copyright © 2005 K.A. Laity

'Raising Lempi' first published in Circle #100 2007. Copyright © 2007 K.A. Laity

'The Kantele' first published in 'Kippis! Literary Jounral' 2009. Copyright © 2009 K.A. Laity

'Raven Sister, Cuckoo Sister', 'Wolf Sister (with drum and night sounds)', 'Vironsusi' and 'Lumottu' Copyright © 2009 K.A. Laity

'Baltic Tango' & 'Confabulation' Copyright © 2015 K.A. Laity

'Confabulation' appeared in the Winter 2015 (and final) edition of New World Finn © 2015 K.A. Laity

About the Author

K. A. Laity is Associate Professor of English at the College of Saint Rose in Albany, New York, where she teaches and writes about medieval literature and culture, popular culture, film, and New Media. She gets her Finnish heritage from her father's side of the family; she grew up in Lansing, Michigan, and spent much time up north at her family's cabin in Kaleva. At present she divides her time between Dundee, Scotland and upstate New York.

Visit K. A. Laity's website: **kalaity.com**

Foxspirit.co.uk

'After nourishment, shelter and companionship, stories are the thing we need most in the world.' Phillip Pullman

Skulk: *noun* – a pack or group of foxes

Fox Spirit believes that day to day life lacks a few things, primarily the fantastic, the magical, the mischievous and even a touch of the horrific. We aim to rectify that by bringing you stories and gorgeous cover art and illustrations from foxy folk who believe as we do that we could all use a little more wonder in our lives.

Here at the Fox Den we believe in storytelling first and foremost, so we mash genres, bend tropes and set fire to rule books merrily as we seek out tall tales that excite and delight us and send them out into the world to find new readers.

With a mixture of established and new writers producing novels, short stories, flash fiction and poetry via ebook and print we recommend letting a little Fox Spirit into your life.

 @foxspiritbooks

 https://www.facebook.com/foxspiritbooks

 adele@foxspirit.co.uk

Printed in Poland
by Amazon Fulfillment
Poland Sp. z o.o., Wrocław

64740546R00123